TH[...]
LAVISH C[...]
BY
STACY-DEANNE
(THE STUDS OF CLEAR CREEK COUNTY)

BOOKS FOR YOUR SOUL

Readers: Thanks so much for choosing my book! I would be very appreciative if you would leave reviews when you are done. Much love!

Email: stacydeanne1@aol.com
Website: Stacy's Website [1]
Facebook: Stacy's Facebook Profile[2]
Twitter: Stacy's Twitter[3]

To receive book announcements subscribe to Stacy's mailing list: Mailing List[4]

---

1.   https://www.stacy-deanne.com/

2.   https://www.facebook.com/stacy.deanne.5

3.   https://twitter.com/stacydeanne

4.   https://stacybooks.eo.page/cjjy6

INTRODUCTION TO CLEAR CREEK COUNTY

Clear Creek County, California (1895): After slavery ended, blacks and whites from the south migrated to California for better opportunities and by the height of the Wild West, the small town of Clear Creek County was 50 percent white and 30 percent black. Most of the males in town (black or white) are uneducated and are ranchers and farmers or working other labor jobs. Affluent white women are the most educated of women in town with the best jobs but the poor and uneducated white women are mostly housewives and depend on their spouses' income. Some are prostitutes who work at the brothel or are "painted ladies" who dance at the saloon.

The skilled black women focus on schooling and higher-class opportunities though they find many challenges in prospering. Still, most black women in Clear Creek County are uneducated and usually become housekeepers and maids. Because of the economic opportunities for black women especially (black maids get higher wages and receive more benefits in CCC than in neighboring towns), more black women are coming to Clear Creek County for a better life but this poses economic challenges for the people already there. Especially other blacks and poor whites already struggling in the town.

Clear Creek County is a small, ranching town where most people know each other or know someone who knows the other. Most are hardworking people who get by on labor, service jobs and ranching. Most of the blacks work for whites. A few work for themselves.

The richest family in Clear Creek County are the Bernsteins who practically own the town. There are several generations of Bernsteins and various families of Bernsteins who call the town home. The next richest family are the Locke family. They are extremely wealthy though not as rich as the Bernsteins and since the Bernsteins discovered Clear

Creek County, the Lockes will never get the same amount of respect but these two families are above all the rest. Like the Bernsteins, there are several Locke households scattered about the town. The Bernsteins and Lockes are the primary employers of every sector in Clear Creek County.

Like any other Wild West town, with fewer opportunities, you have some who step outside of the law to survive either out of obligation or desire. There are outlaws, crime, and disruption.

Clear Creek County is not a perfect place. But for the characters spotlighted in this series, it is home and they cherish it with all their hearts.

This series focuses on the journey between various black heroines trying to build a life in Clear Creek County and the men they fall in love with. Each book stands alone focusing on original characters and different plots. Some characters such as Sheriff Angus Snow and the Duke Brothers are recurring and you will see them throughout the series if not every book. Concerning other characters, some will pop up again as needed and some you will never see beyond the book they were first mentioned.

Enjoy!

BOOKMARK THIS LINK TO KEEP UP WITH NEW RELEASES IN THE SERIES:
   https://bit.ly/3Tdl4CQ

CHAPTER ONE

Clear Creek County, California
1895

"Oh!" Fiona Acres stumbled, her black lace-up boots getting stuck on the dusty road as three white men on horses burst through the woods and surrounded her.

Squeezing the handle of her leather suitcase, Fiona turned in a circle, looking at the men one-by-one.

"You new here, right?" The somewhat handsome one with the brown cowboy hat spit tobacco juice. "Yeah, ain't never seen *you* before. Where you going, gal?"

"Hey, Kit." The chubbier redheaded guy straightened his horse. "Bet she another Negro from Braesville coming to be a maid."

The threesome laughed, spitting simultaneously.

"Maybe." Fiona stuck her chin in the air. "Maybe not. I don't see what business it is of *yours*."

The one called Kit raised his eyebrows. "What did you say to me, gal?"

"I think you heard me, sir. Now, if you excuse me, I need to be on my way."

The men blocked her with their horses.

"Yeah." The black-haired one with the spectacles grimaced. "You must be from Braesville, talkin' to us like that. Negroes sure are uppity there."

"Yeah, well, we gonna fix that." Kit massaged his large gloved hands. "In case you don't get it, this here is Clear Creek County and you better remember your place or I'm gonna show it to you. Now where you going and I ain't asking again."

She tried to walk around the fat guy's horse, but he stayed in place. "I'm going to work for Charlie Bernstein."

4

"Bernsteins." The spectacles guy scoffed. "So sick of them and the Lockes bringing in these out-of-town niggers."

"So I was right?" Kit smirked. "You gonna be a maid? Bending down on your hands and knees? Messing up your back? How old are you?"

Fiona sighed. "Twenty-one."

The men whistled.

"Young." Kit licked his lips. "And ripe, huh? And pretty decent looking for a nigger."

Fiona held her breath to keep from swatting him with her suitcase, but that wouldn't have been a good idea no matter where she was.

"You could make a lot of money, gal." Kit leaned forward, squinting. "Come see Carl Lansing for a *real* job."

"Who's Carl Lansing?"

"Just a businessman." Kit sat up straight, his horse wiggling. "A very *resourceful* businessman."

"Carl's talent is making money," the redheaded guy said. "And helping others as well."

Kit scowled. "You really wanna be scraping by working for the Bernsteins?"

"Why not?" Fiona wiggled her shoulders. "It's an honest living unlike what you're talking about."

Kit shrugged. "What do you *think* we're talking about?"

"Come on." Fiona batted her long lashes. "I might've just come from Braesville, but I ain't been living under a rock. We got men like Carl Lansing, too."

Spectacles snickered. "What do you mean by that?"

"It's easy to tell he's doing stuff under the table," Fiona said. "I mean, if *you* guys work for him, then that's a given."

The men groaned as they looked at each other.

"I don't want no part of what you guys are selling." Fiona rushed away from them but once again, they blocked her.

"You don't get it," Kit said. "We ain't asking."

"Maybe *you* don't get it, sir." Fiona smiled. "But I ain't interested in working with this Carl Lansing. Please leave me alone."

Kit jumped off his horse. "I'm sick of your ass already." He snatched her suitcase.

"Hey!" Fiona lunged at him but the guy with the glasses hopped off his horse and grabbed her. "Give me my bag!"

"Damn, look at this thing, Kit!" Redhead examined Fiona's worn luggage. "Looks older
than dirt. Ha, ha!"

"Stop it!" Fiona jumped and reached while the men tossed the suitcase over her head and
around her. "Give me my suitcase!" She lunged at Kit, who threw it to the redhead guy again. "Leave me alone!"

"Hey, leave her alone!" This teeny-tiny Negro girl with her hair sticking all over her head flew from across the road, in a thin linen dress and barefoot. "Get away from her, Kit!"

"Go on, girl." He got in her face. "You better get out of here, Lovely Jo!"

The petite woman turned to Fiona, sweating and panting. "I'm Lovely Jo. You is?"

"Um, Fiona Acres. I just got here from Braesville."

"Wish I could say you'll enjoy it here." Lovely Jo rolled her eyes at Kit. "But as you can see, there's a couple of assholes runnin' around the place."

Fiona chuckled.

"Give it back, Kit!" Lovely Jo jumped up and down, reaching for the suitcase. "Come on. Ain't you too old for this?"

"You better get outta here, gal!" He pushed her to the ground. "Get out the hell out of here, Lovely Jo!"

"Naw, the sheriff, right down the road. I'll go get him!" Lovely Jo ran off like lightning. "Just hold on, Miss Fiona!"

Laughing, the men continued with their childish torturing.

"Come on, girl." Kit dangled the suitcase in front of Fiona like she was a dog. "Come and get it. Come *on*."

"You bastards! Give me my suitcase!"

Kit pushed her. "Come and get it, bitch—"

"Kit!"

The men stopped, their grins frozen on their faces.

An older man with silver hair, silver beard and his badge stuck on his belt underneath this pot belly, rode up on his horse with a mousy much younger man riding his own horse behind him.

"Ah, hell." Kit groaned, snatching Fiona's suitcase from the guy with the glasses. "Sheriff Snow. How you doing today?"

"Fine." Snow squinted underneath his hat. "What are *you* doing, Kit? Besides being a nuisance with yourself, as usual?"

"A nuisance, Sheriff?" Kit smirked. "That ain't nice."

"They took my bag." Fiona pointed to Kit. "And won't give it back. I just wanna be on my way."

Snow tossed his eagle-like gaze from Fiona to Kit. "That looks like one of them ladies' suitcases, Kit. Not exactly yo' style. Why don't you give it back and be on your way?"

"We ain't mean no harm." Kit tossed Fiona the bag. "Wanted to welcome her to Clear Creek County."

The other men snickered.

"The best welcome you can give her is to get going." Sheriff spit. "About now."

Kit bowed to Fiona. "I meant no harm, ma'am."

She hugged her suitcase to her chest.

"Hope you enjoy your stay in our lovely town." With that smug smile, Kit jumped on his horse and the three rode off in the opposite direction.

"You okay, ma'am?" the younger guy asked. "Oh, this is Sheriff Snow and I'm Mason." He beamed with pride. "His deputy."

"T... thank you." Fiona watched Kit and the men fade in the dust. "They come out of
nowhere."

"You handle yourself pretty good," Snow said. "Kit's just a bunch of talk. He came out of his momma bullying girls. Pay him no mind."

Mason straightened his horse. "What's your name, Miss?"

"Fiona Acres. I come from Braesville." She pointed behind her. "Just got dropped off and was minding my business when them guys popped outta the wood like weeds. Was talking about some guy named Carl Lansing?"

Snow groaned. "That's another one you'll wanna stay away from. Ain't nothing good come from no Carl Lansing."

"They said he had a job I might want, but I knew it was bad news."

"Yeah, Lansing is nothing you wanna be messin' with," Mason said. "You sure don't want no job he's offering."

"Oh, believe me, sir. I have no intent on ever talking to this Lansing. I'm going to be working for the Bernsteins."

"Which ones?" Mason grinned. "They're about a hundred of them here."

"Charlie Bernstein."

"Ah, Charlie." Dust fell from Snow's beard as he scratched it. "You ain't too far away. Want a ride? That way you don't have to worry about Kit and the fellas showing up again."

"Yes." Fiona exhaled. "I'd appreciate that."

"Hop on with Mason." Snow turned his horse around. "We'll get you to Charlie's before you can blink."

****

Fiona was glad to see that at least some myths about Clear Creek County seemed true. For example, folks said the whites were more tolerable to coloreds and, by the nice way Sheriff Snow and Mason treated her, it seemed accurate. She'd not hold Kit and those thugs against the town, for you had troublemakers everywhere, but Snow and Mason's kindness reiterated her coming to Clear Creek County for a better life might've been the best decision after all.

"See that, Miss Fiona?" Mason pointed to the wooden mansion up ahead with its sharp towers and grand architecture. "That's Charlie's mansion."

"My *Lord*. I've never seen a place so grand."

"Welcome to the rich of the rich," Snow said. "The Bernsteins practically own Clear Creek County."

"What is Charlie like?" Fiona struggled to hold her suitcase. "Is he nice?"

Sheriff Snow grinned at Mason.

"What?" Fiona asked. "Did I say something funny, sir?"

"Oh, Charlie's nice all right," Mason said. "Especially to beautiful women. So I suspect you and him will get along just fine."

Fiona sighed. She'd heard some things about Charlie's appetite for women and had hoped they weren't all true. She wanted a job not to be some white man's concubine. If that ended up the case, she'd be back in Braesville so fast her head would spin.

"I just wanna work." Fiona cleared her throat. "I'm a respectable woman."

"Don't worry, Miss Fiona," Mason said. "Charlie wouldn't pressure you into nothin'. He just like women a lot is all but what man don't? He ain't gonna be indecent with ya.'"

"That is, of course..." Snow spit. "Unless you give him a chance to."

Fiona sat back, holding her breath as they got to the iron gate that separated the mansion
from the road.

"Here we are." Mason smiled at Fiona from over his shoulder. "Glad we could help you, ma'am."

"Hey there, Sheriff! Mason!" A Negro with a bushy beard who looked like a building with arms and legs threw a log on a pile of lumber. "How y'all doing today?"

Fiona gaped. "Oh... my... God."

"That's Big Pearl," Mason said. "He a biggin, ain't he?"

Fiona did a double take. "And then some."

"Big Pearl," Snow said. "You working for Charlie now?"

"Yes, sir." He stomped over in his giant overalls, his crispy wild hair sticking up over his round head. "Hey there." He smiled at Fiona with them big yellow eyes looking like lanterns in windows. "I'm Big Pearl." He stuck out his huge chest as if she was supposed to know who he was. "Who are you?"

"Fiona." She looked him over, from his boots to his head. "Man. You a buildin' ain't ya'?"

Big Pearl laughed, his entire body shaking.

"Big Pearl is a gentle giant," Snow said. "Unless you make him mad and you don't wanna make him mad."

"Hello." Fiona took Big Pearl's ashy hand and his swallowed hers. "Nice to meet you, Big Pearl."

"You too, ma'am. You coming in from Braesville, I reckon?"

She nodded.

"Got any family here?"

"No. Just coming on my own to work for the Bernsteins."

Sweat flew off Big Pearl's forehead. "Oh, you'll like working for Mr. Charlie. He don't bother you none. He a businessman. It's Miss Sue Ann you gotta worry about she—"

"Big Pearl!" A young woman who seemed slightly older than Fiona swaggered off the veranda as if she didn't know how to use her legs. "Big Pearl! We don't pay you to jibber jabber. Get back to work!"

CHAPTER TWO

"Oh, Lord," Mason said to Fiona. "That's Miss Sue Ann. Charlie's younger sister."

"You talkin' about pitiful." Snow shook his head. "It's a shame, but she like a rose dipped in mud. A waste of all that prettiness."

"Big Pearl." Sue Ann belched. "You hear me, boy?"

"Yes, Miss Sue Ann." He hurried his huge self back to the lumber. "I'm bringing out the wood, Miss Sue Ann. I'll be right back." He rushed behind the house.

Sue Ann wobbled to the gate and held onto it. "You must be the new gal from Braesville." She batted her woozy blue eyes. "I'm Miss Sue Ann Bernstein and don't you forget it."

"Yes, ma'am." Fiona nodded. "I swear I won't forget it. I'm Fiona Acres. Nice to meet you, Miss Sue Ann."

Sue Ann gulped as if she were about to throw up. "It sure is hot out here today."

"Uh, Sue Ann, you okay?" Mason asked. "Looks like you've had a lot to drink already."

"Mind your business!" She slammed her eyes shut, stumbling. "I'm doing just fine, thank you, very much. Hey, gal?"

Fiona batted her eyes.

"Welcome to Clear Creek County." Sue Ann rolled her eyes and stumbled back into the house.

"I ain't never seen a woman that drunk before," Fiona said.

Snow snickered. "You working here now, you gonna get used to it."

Just as Sue Ann went back inside, a tall, skinny white woman who looked at least in her 60s tottered out in a long black maid's dress with a white apron and her collar past her long neck. She walked to the carriage with her little head bobbing as if someone had stuck it on a stick.

"Sheriff." She held her skirt as she walked off the steps. "Mason."

"Miss Mildred." Sheriff Snow tipped his hat and Fiona swore he was blushing a bit. He and Miss Mildred seemed around the same age, so it wouldn't have surprised Fiona if Snow was a little sweet on the woman.

"So." Miss Mildred walked to Mason's horse and stood with her feet together and back erect as if she were preparing for battle. "You must be Miss Fiona Acres. I'm Miss Mildred. The head housekeeper."

"Miss Mildred." Fiona plastered on a smile as she shook Mildred's wrinkled, bony hand. "It's nice to meet you, ma'am."

"Hm." Mildred looked Fiona over with tight lips. "You're pretty, huh?"

Fiona looked at Snow, who smiled back at her.

"That might be a problem," Mildred said in a stiff voice that reminded Fiona of what wood might sound like if it could talk.

"Um, why would that be a problem, Miss Mildred?"

"Because Charlie likes pretty things." She squinted, every wrinkle drawing toward her eyes. "And that can cause trouble when business is mixed with pleasure. Not to mention, the colored maid fornicating with the master of the house is not something Miss Katherine would approve of."

"Miss Katherine." Fiona hugged her suitcase. "That's Charlie's mother, right?"

"Charlie owns this house now. The business as well." Mildred looked back at the mansion, nodding. "His Pa gave Charlie everything before he died but Miss Katherine, well you still gotta respect her and she don't want no messing around between you and Charlie."

"Oh, no." Fiona shook her head. "I'm a decent woman, I assure you. All I wanna do is my job and nothing else."

"Well, come on then, let's skedaddle." Mildred clapped her hands. "We don't have time to waste. You got a lot of work to do."

Fiona struggled as she got off Mason's horse. "Thanks so much for the ride."

Mason nodded. "You're welcome, Miss Fiona."

"Let's go!" Mildred pulled a stumbling Fiona up the veranda stairs and into the mansion.

Nonstop, Mildred talked from the moment Fiona stepped foot inside.

Like the exterior, the inside of the mansion was just as intimidating. Full of polished wood, the walls were covered in paintings or wallpaper with golden stripes and motifs.

Mildred barked instructions concerning Fiona's daily duties while leading Fiona up the winding stairs and onto the second floor which boasted more luxury.

Crystal hung from the ceilings. Gold glimmered from the corners. Even the rooms smelled of wood, warm and earthy.

A chill hit Fiona the minute Mildred showed her to her room in the servants' quarters. It

reminded Fiona she was farther from home than she first realized.

"This is your room." Mildred scampered about the large bedroom, which wasn't as fancy as the other rooms in the house but certainly better than the one-room log cabin Fiona had grown up in with eight sisters and brothers.

Not to mention her dog, Fluffy.

"Well." Mildred stood on the rug with her hands clasped behind her back, chin in the air. "What do you think?"

"It's amazing." Fiona took off her sunbonnet and laid it on the white linen sheet. She walked around, touching the polished wood of the bookshelf, admiring the little window. "We didn't have a window at my house." She looked out of it, seeing the massive forest that surrounded Charlie's home. "This room looks too good for a maid."

"Then I suspect you're grateful."

"Oh, yes, ma'am." Fiona rushed back to Mildred. "I am ever so grateful. I appreciate all the kindness you've shown me so far."

"Mm-hmm." Mildred's pointy lips got even tighter. "Since I've told you about the place and your duties, you should know more about the family. Charlie is a hound dog."

Fiona sat on the bed. "A hound dog, Miss?"

"I told you he likes pretty things, and that's an understatement. Hopefully he minds his manners with you, but I can't promise you anything." Mildred wiggled her shoulders. "He is a man in a position of extreme wealth and power, so to him, anything goes. He won't force himself on you, though. That's not Charlie's way."

Fiona exhaled, touching her full bosom. "I'm relieved to hear that."

"But don't be surprised if he puts his desires on you." Mildred sighed. "Just seems a shame for a Negro to be so pretty. Just a waste."

Fiona broke eye contact.

"Sue Ann is Charlie's younger sister. Twenty-five and pitiful." Mildred shook her head. "She's a chore to understand, that one. She's beautiful, but a mess."

"Sheriff Snow said she was a rose in mud."

Mildred nodded. "Perfect way to describe her. She does nothing to make herself desirable or even tolerable. Just drinks. See, she's Leonard Bernstein's bastard child. After Leonard died, Charlie and Katherine took pity on her, so they invited her to stay."

"Miss Sue Ann is Charlie's father's daughter?"

Mildred nodded. "Leonard wanted nothing to do with her when he was alive, so she has a chip on her shoulder and unfortunately everyone in this house is paying for it. Sue Ann should've been an actress. She plays so many parts you never know who the real her is."

"I could smell the liquor from when she was standing on the porch."

Mildred wiggled her shoulders. "She stays in her room a lot. Claims she wants to be a part of the family but never says anything nice, only picks fights with Charlie and Katherine."

"Seems like she's hurting from something."

"Sue Ann's a grown woman now and needs to get over the past." Mildred straightened the vase of flowers on the dressing table. "She's a Bernstein, but she does nothing to take advantage of the privilege. People would kill for what she has. My advice is just to ignore her."

Fiona muttered, "Something tells me that won't be so easy."

CHAPTER THREE

Charlie didn't give Fiona Acres another thought when he first heard she was coming to Clear Creek County. Just another Negro woman looking for yet another job. That's what he thought until he saw her.

Staring down at her from the upstairs window in his study, he welcomed the distraction. He hadn't imagined she'd be so beautiful. She put even the white ladies who spent every waking moment painting their faces and buying the best dresses to shame. Now, before she came, he wouldn't have thought of making a move but with this impending business deal on his mind, he craved relaxation and going out with Jane Locke and playing the "wooing" game was anything but. He was exhausted.

Tired of life. Tired of being a Bernstein and doing what they expected of him. In thirty-four years, he'd never once lived his own life.

Fiona walked through the garden, sniffing flowers but none of them compared to the flower he stared at. She wasn't just a maid coming to do a job to support her family. She was his fate. He felt it in his heart. God sent her to him for a reason. To rescue him from this mundane life. To show him he was his own man underneath the Bernstein name and riches.

Fiona was different because she wouldn't care about status. He wouldn't need to impress her or spend hours figuring out what he'd say before meeting with her. No. He could just be himself. She was a maid. In fact, *his* maid, so she couldn't expect anything from him he wasn't willing to give. She wasn't a socialite like Jane Locke. Someone he had to be on his guard with at all times. A woman who demanded to be treated like a queen.

No. Fiona didn't expect any of that. Charlie could probably just flash a smile or say hello to her and it would make Fiona's day. Because despite how stunning she was, she wouldn't be getting much attention beyond these walls.

So with her, Charlie didn't have to play the part. He could be carefree. Make mistakes, Be unprepared.

He smirked as his erection punctured the seat of his pants.

He could have fun with her. No strings attached. No pressure.

With Fiona, maybe, just maybe, he could forget what it meant to be a Bernstein.

At least for a little while.

****

Everyone else probably thought Charlie's home was a marvel because of the elegance that clung to every room and the expensive trinkets. But what made this home fascinating to Fiona was the library in the lounge.

Fiona loved books. Cherished them. Her parents couldn't read and it had been up to her and her older sister to teach the younger siblings. Fiona wouldn't have made it past the age of 10 without books. No way she'd have gotten through the pain and hopelessness of poverty if not for the ability to escape through literature.

She loved many books, but romance was her favorite because though her sister teased her about dreaming, Fiona always wished some handsome stranger would come sweep her away. Sure, she wasn't a dignified white heroine with endless prospects like the women she read about, but one thing society couldn't take away from her was her dreams.

Les Miserables.

The name stuck out to her, though she didn't know how to pronounce it. She read the description on the back cover.

"That's my favorite book."

"Oh!" Fiona turned, dropping the book.

Charlie Bernstein leaned up against the doorframe, smirking, yet his smile wasn't as annoying as Kit's was. "You dropped something."

"Mr. Bernstein." She hurriedly picked up the book. "I'm sorry. You... well, you startled me."

"I figured."

He didn't fit the playboy persona at first glance. Oh, he definitely had the charm and good looks to turn a woman's life upside down, but he didn't flaunt it like you'd suspect.

His eyes struck Fiona the most. Sharp and blue, they distracted you from whatever secret he might've been hiding.

"That's my favorite book," he repeated. "Les Miserables."

Her heart fluttered when he sang the word so eloquently.

"I like the main character." He walked as if he knew he owned the world and he wanted you to know it, too. "See, he changed and made a better life for himself despite others not believing in him." His stare cut through Fiona as he slipped the book from her fingers, touching her on purpose.

"The best characters are those who remind us of ourselves."

Fiona swallowed, turning away from his suffocating gaze. "I apologize, sir. I should be cleaning and not fiddling about. That's not what you pay me for."

"Beautiful women should never apologize."

Fiona shivered. "You think I'm beautiful?"

"Please don't play that game where you act like you don't know how attractive you are." He rolled his eyes. "I hate it when people play modest."

"I know I'm beautiful." Fiona stuck her chin in the air. "It's just that white men rarely admit a Negro woman is beautiful."

"Well, I guess I'm not the average white man."

She grinned.

He had thick wavy hair as black as a raven's feathers, but unlike other men in Clear Creek County, not even stubble on his face. Just those long sideburns, which seemed pointless, with no beard or mustache.

"What do you know about Les Miserables?"

She chuckled. "Only what you've told me. I'd spend weeks trying to pronounce the name if you hadn't."

He snickered, his Roman nose wiggling. "What do you like to read?"

"Um, romances."

He squinted, his pronounced cheekbones flexing. "Why romances?"

"Because they're fantasy yet realistic at the same time."

"Tell." He crossed his arms over that wide chest while straightening his broad shoulders. "What do you mean by that?"

"Romances present a world you can dream about yet have at the same time. Like, the hero is larger-than-life. You most likely will never meet a man like that. That's the fantasy part. But you can meet a man who loves you and makes you happier than you've ever been. That's the realistic part."

"Hm." Charlie pulled his bottom lip. "Have you ever met a man like that, Miss Fiona?"

She swallowed, suddenly feeling thirsty. It was a thirst she never felt before, like no amount of water would ever quench it. The feeling got worse the longer he looked at her. She had to turn away or else she'd have fainted because looking at him, well, it took her breath away.

"Miss Fiona?" He moved even closer to her. "Ever met a man like that?"

"Some might find this strange, Mr. Charlie. Most employers don't have time to talk to the maid."

"Guess I'm gonna have to show you to stop comparing me to others, huh?" He snickered. "I'm betting I am unlike any man you've ever met. You'll never be able to guess my actions, so don't try."

"I wouldn't dream of that, sir."

"Other than romances?" He uncrossed his arms. "What else do you like to read?"

"I like Phyllis Wheatley."

"So you like poetry?" His face brightened. "She has such a way with words. Is that why you like her?"

"You read colored poets?"

"Why should her being Negro matter? It's her talent that's important. I don't care what color she is." He tilted his head. "Why do you like her? For the gift she has of evoking emotion with a simple passage of words?"

She grinned. "I like her because she's colored."

He laughed. "At least you're honest."

"I learn through her experiences from her work. It's good to have writers Negroes can relate to."

"You went to school?"

"My older sister went to school, and she taught me how to read and do math. Contrary to popular belief, many Negroes like education and love to learn."

"I apologize." He stood back. "I wasn't meaning to offend—"

"Oh, no, Mr. Charlie. I'm sorry if I offended *you*. You did nothing wrong."

"If I ever do anything to offend, let me know. I don't want you to be afraid to be honest, thinking I'll fire you or something."

"No, sir." She nodded. "And, yes, sir, I'll be honest if that's the case." She smiled. "But you've done nothing wrong. I'm happy you're so interested."

"I am indeed."

They stared at each other and Fiona was shocked she was still standing. She couldn't feel

her legs, nothing but the beating of her heart, and it seemed to get louder the more Charlie looked

at her.

"If you'll forgive me, Mr. Charlie, I have to finish my work." She fluttered past him. "Miss Mildred has a ton of things she needs me to get to."

He whisked around. "Are you a virgin, Miss Fiona?"

She stayed facing the door, her nerves crushing her ribcage. "What?"

"Are you a virgin?" He walked up behind her and she stiffened up like a wall. "Might be improper to ask, but I'd like to know."

"I'm saving myself for marriage. Like any decent woman would, sir."

He pressed up against her and lowered his head to where he whispered into her ear, "*Pity.*"

Holding his hands behind his back, Charlie strutted out of the room.

CHAPTER FOUR

"Wilber, the deal's going through. Do you doubt me?" Charlie walked around his study, talking into the candlestick phone. "West Pine will be the perfect place to build the hotel. I can see it now." He sat on his desk of polished wood. "First it starts with hotels and then we get more restaurants. Then hospitals and before you know it, Clear Creek County will be the biggest little town around." He laughed. "Trust me. Everything's fine."

"You forgetting one thing?" Wilber sighed. "The coloreds? The Negroes who live on West Pine? We can't build over them, Charlie."

"Minor discrepancies." He smirked. "What we say goes. They can't fight us. Plus, I'm a Bernstein and my family owns this town."

"I don't know. I want to see this through, but throwing all those people out on the streets? There's families and kids, Charlie."

"Wilber, are you really gonna let Negroes ruin this operation? You know what my father taught me?" He stood. "That in order to get things done, you gotta step on some people. Now I don't like it, but I'm not gonna jeopardize this deal for nobody. This is my time to prove I can run the business better than my father. We'll give the Negroes some money to start over. But beyond that, it's not our problem."

"You're right." Wilber snickered. "That hotel will bring a lot of revenue into Clear Creek County."

"That's right." Charlie got his pipe. "This will be the biggest deal I've pulled off since Papa died. I refuse to fail."

"I bet your daddy's smiling down on you from Heaven."

Charlie looked at the floor. "I was thinking of a place a little lower."

They guffawed.

****

A few days later, Big Pearl slumped past Fiona as she was cleaning the windows by the front door.

"Oh, hey, Big Pearl." She dipped her rag into the mixture of vinegar and water. "You look mighty low today. Are you okay?"

"Nah." He fidgeted, looking as though he didn't know which direction to go in. "I gotta finish fixing the shed out back. I don't wanna bother you with my problems."

"Well, you ain't bothering me, Big Pearl, if I asked." Fiona circled the damp rag on the window. "What's going on?"

"Somebody is threatening folks over in West Pine."

"That's one of the colored areas, ain't it?"

"Yeah." He hooked his thumbs in the pockets of his overalls. "My family live there and my parents got this note telling them it's best they get out and don't make a fuss or they'll regret it. From Garrett Associates. It's a law firm."

"Wait, a law firm said your parents gotta move?"

"Yeah, they sent a letter to the whole doggone neighborhood. Miss Fiona, that's the oldest colored neighborhood in Clear Creek County and the note says it's been sold and we gotta all be gone in the next six months. What we gonna do?"

"They can't do that, Big Pearl." Fiona held her waist. "You can't just kick folks out of their homes."

"You forgettin' we colored?" He huffed. "They can do anything they want, but we gotta fight this."

"Well you gonna, ain't you?"

"Course I will. My whole family live in that house and I got my wife and baby girl there too. Man, I just can't believe this. Everything was finally looking up for me. I finally got another job and now my family home's gonna be ripped away from us. I heard from the grapevine they want the land to build hotels there."

"Who wants the land?"

"Some company." He shrugged. "Hell, I don't know. Can't find any info on them."

"Big Pearl, listen." Fiona touched his shoulder. "Colored or not, there are laws. They cannot just take someone's land and kick them out. You have rights. Ain't there some colored lawyer or someone you can talk to?"

He scratched his beard. "The only colored lawyer is outside of Clear Creek County."

"That's who you gotta talk to, then." Fiona went back to cleaning. "You can't give up, Big Pearl. Gotta stand up and fight. They want us to back down. I'll keep my eyes and ears open for you too, okay? Say, maybe Mr. Charlie could help. He's a Bernstein."

"Nah, I don't wanna bother him with my nonsense—"

"Big Pearl!" Katherine Bernstein marched her short, stocky body off the stairs. "Boy, how come every time I see you, you talking? You do more talking than working."

"I'm sorry, Miss Katherine." He rushed to the front door. "I'm getting to the shed right now. You need anything else?"

"All I need is for you to get back to work." She bobbed her head full of short grayish-blonde curls. "Skedaddle."

"Yes, ma'am. See you later, Fiona."

She grinned. "All right, Big Pearl."

He slammed the door so hard he knocked a portrait off the wall.

"Good Lord." Katherine picked it up and put it back in its place. "Since he's been here he's broken glasses, lanterns, vases. It's a wonder we still have walls."

"Miss Katherine. Do you know Garrett Associates?"

"Course." She straightened the portrait. "Leonard worked with them a few times for business. Why?"

"They sent Big Pearl's family a letter on behalf of someone threatening to take Big Pearl's family home."

Katherine clutched her pearls. "What?"

"Really, they wanna run all the coloreds out of West Pine. Something about the land's being sold and they wanna build on it."

"My God." Katherine scowled. "Now I ain't business minded, but I know this ain't right. You shouldn't take nobody's land. You know the name of the company?"

Fiona shook her head. "It's heartbreaking. Them people work so hard and now to have someone take their land like this?"

"I'll talk to Charlie about it." Katherine's forehead sprouted wrinkles. "Maybe he knows what's going on but business deals, well men keep them away from the women folk so I doubt any of my friends would know. I'll mention it to Charlie, okay?"

"Thanks, Miss Katherine."

"Yeah." She grinned as she pointed to the window. "And you get back to work, Missy."

****

Fiona couldn't let the West Pine thing go. It wasn't her business, but she felt Negroes needed
    to stick together. Plus, she was afraid that if this was allowed in West Pine, then people would start thinking it was okay to take all the colored folks' land. Then where would they be? Back to being property like during slavery?

After asking another maid where Charlie was, Fiona found him on the patio in the garden, reading as always. Holding her breath, she approached, but she hated to interrupt him. Every time he read, his eyes lit up with so much joy. Reminded her of a little boy with a brand new pony.

"Fiona." He lowered the book, smiling. "What a pleasant surprise." He took a puff from his pipe. "Something I can do for you?"

"Something has been bothering me awful." She rubbed her hands together. "It ain't really my business, but I feel I got a duty to be concerned, you know? May I sit down, sir?"

"Of course."

She sat in the wooden chair with the handmade cushion in the seat. "I love your chairs. Feel so comfortable, like when your momma holds your bottom when you a baby."

His hairline rose. "That's an interesting analogy, Miss Fiona. What's troubling you?"

"You know who Garrett Associates is?"

"Let me guess. Is this about Big Pearl's family?" Charlie sucked the pipe. "Ma told me about it and I said I'd look into it." His gaze shifted. "I'll do that as soon as I can, but understand I'm a busy man dealing with Bernstein business."

"Oh, I completely understand, Mr. Charlie. Whenever you can get to it, that's fine. I'm sure it'll give Big Pearl and the others hope that you're on their side."

His eyes twinkled and looked more green than blue in the sun. "Uh, it's nice to see you so concerned. Most wouldn't care about something that didn't affect *them*."

CHAPTER FIVE

"But it affects me," Fiona said. "Negroes gotta stick together and what would make them stop at one neighborhood? This is disgusting, Mr. Charlie. It really is. Taking the homes of hardworking people who never did nothing to nobody."

"Is life black and white to you, Miss Fiona?"

She batted her eyes. "Sir?"

"Do you just see good and bad, or do you see in between? Have you stopped to think about the people doing this? Any positives that might come from it?"

"What positives could come from kicking families off their land, sir?"

"I'm not saying it's neat. But there's two sides to every coin. Like, this hotel will bring in a lot of jobs for Negros, especially."

"So it's a hotel they want built?" She scoffed. "They wanna kick folks out their homes to build hotels. Irony."

He raised an eyebrow. "Irony, huh?"

"I don't care why they are doing it, it's wrong. And these people already have jobs. They don't need to be thrown out of their homes for jobs. I'm pretty sure if you asked them what they'd rather have, they'd pick the life they have now."

Charlie sat back, slowly moving the pipe in and out of his lips.

"We was homeless at one point." Fiona sat erect. "Me and my family. Papa lost his job and for a while there, we had nowhere to lay our heads and didn't know where our next meal was coming from. I don't know how we got through that period but by the grace of God we did it and I said then, enemy or not, if I could help someone to not have to feel the pain of not having a place to stay, I would."

Charlie's eyes watered as he swallowed.

"It's a pain I can't describe." Fiona sniffled. "To not belong anywhere. To feel as unimportant as a leaf on a tree. A house is more than a structure, Mr. Charlie. It's life. It's family. It's children. It's love. It's memories. How can anyone take that away from another person? What monsters could do something like that?"

He dropped his gaze.

"So when you say there are two sides, yeah, but one is wrong. And I'll never change my
mind on that."

"I'm sorry for what you've been through, Miss Fiona. It's only makes you even more remarkable."

She sat at attention. "Remarkable?"

"Yes. I admire you for what you did. Coming down here alone and unmarried to make a life for yourself. To support your family. Alone in a strange place. Don't know nobody. Even I could never do that." He leaned forward and touched her hand. "You're a light, Miss Fiona. And you shine brighter than the sun above. And I see you." He squeezed her hand. "I see the woman you are inside and out. And I wanna know her. Every part—"

"Mr. Charlie." She stood. "Uh, I—"

"I'm sorry." His brow furrowed. "I didn't mean to make you uncomfortable."

She panted, rubbing the spot on her hand he'd touched.

"Or maybe I *didn't* make you uncomfortable?" His eyes turned to half moons. "Maybe you're feeling something else, Miss Fiona? Something I'm feeling right now?"

"I'm feeling confusion, sir." She stood behind the chair. "And we need to nip it in the bud."

"I'm the employer here. I say when we nip something in the bud, and maybe right now I don't want to." He frowned. "Maybe I like the feeling you give me. Maybe I wanna keep feeling it. Wanna explore—"

"You told me in the library to be honest with you. Well, I am now. Please, Mr. Charlie, I don't wanna go down this route. I got a lot riding on this, and I can't let anything jeopardize my job."

"You think I'd do that, Fiona?"

"I don't know what you'd do. All I know is we can't do *this*." She held the back of the chair. "Things get complicated when feelings get involved. And that don't bring nothing but trouble, especially in situations like these."

"I like trouble." He licked his lips. "Trouble is exciting. Trouble is what I don't get enough of, Miss Fiona."

"With all due respect, sir. You should get in trouble with a woman of your own station." She looked down. "And your own color."

"Well, in case no one has mentioned this to you, Miss Fiona, we can't control who we wanna

get in trouble with. Unless you know something I don't—"

"*Fiona*!" Mildred yelled her name in that high-pitched squealing that could split eardrums. "Fiona, where are you, girl?"

"I'm coming, Miss Mildred!" Fiona dashed from the table. "I gotta go, Mr. Charlie."

He stood. "Come back to the garden tonight! So we can talk again."

"I... I gotta go!"

Fiona ran into the house.

****

Two Weeks Later

Charlie was what Fiona's daddy would've called slick. At first, he was so gentlemanly with her. Patient. But lately he'd gotten more aggressive with trying to spend time with her and she'd done her absolute best to avoid him. He'd pop from around corners. Sneak up on her as she came out of her room. He even tried to get her to go to town with him, and she faked sick. Stayed in her room all day just to not be near him.

She was determined with all her might not to fall into any trap with Charlie Bernstein, for it would ruin her existence like nothing else.

But he was a conning man and the more she resisted, the more he kept going. She never knew what Charlie would try next. Everything he did seemed to be to test her. To see how far he could push her before she gave in. One thing he hadn't done, at least not yet, was force himself on her, but she had to be honest with herself on that one. If he tried, would it really be by force after all? When she wanted him so much?

But Charlie seemed obsessed. Wanting to be by Fiona always even if she wasn't speaking to him. He'd even made a rule that Fiona had to stay in the dining room while the family ate dinner. So she stood in the back quietly every night watching the Bernstein show and she found it quite entertaining. Sue Ann never missed a beat. Say what you wanted to about Sue Ann Bernstein but you couldn't say she wasn't funny as hell.

"Shut up, Charlie." Sue Ann bounced in her chair like a child. "I want a drink and I'm gonna get one. Fiona, get me a drink!"

"Yes, ma'am."

"Fiona, don't you dare move from that spot." Charlie glared at his unruly sister. "Sue Ann

done had enough."

"It ain't never enough, Big Brother." She looked at Katherine, who shook her head while eating as if she'd rather be anywhere but there. "All I want is a drink around here! Is that too much to ask?" Sue Ann banged her fists on the table. "Ain't that what the help is for? To get me what I need?"

"I've about had it!" Charlie threw his fork at her.

"Oh, God." Katherine covered her face.

"That's it, Sue Ann!" Charlie pointed at her, a fat vein popping out of his neck. "I'm tired of your shenanigans. We brought you into this house out of love and compassion and all you do is take, take, take!"

"Love and compassion? Ha!" She whipped her head until her crinkles covered her face. "Can we please stop this act, Charlie? You and Katherine letting me stay here ain't about no love or compassion.

It's about you feeling guilty because Daddy gave you everything under the sun and me nothing!"

"You a liar, Sue Ann!" Katherine turned red. "You a liar! Leonard sent your momma money. He done right by you the best he could."

"Oh, *really*?" Sue Ann clenched her bouncy white bosom, which hung out of her dress. "Let's see, uh. I must've gotten mixed up, Katherine. Where was all this love and concerned from Daddy Leonard? I can't remember the man seeing me but once when I fell ill, and I heard that's because you told him to!"

"He seen you plenty of times," Katherine barked. "You was just too young to remember."

"I remember everything about my childhood, Katherine." Sue Ann wiggled her neck. "I remember living in that crummy hut that wasn't even fit for a family of rats while Charlie grew up with a silver spoon in his mouth."

Charlie groaned as he cut into his steak.

"Growing up eating steak." Sue Ann picked up her plate and slammed it back on the silk table cloth. "Having this huge home to run around in. This motif wallpaper, crystals and gold. While me and my momma was hidden away in that heap because Leonard Bernstein was too ashamed to let anyone know he'd played around on his wife and had a daughter!"

"That's it!" Katherine slammed her fork down. "Get out of here, Sue Ann! I don't wanna see

your face anymore tonight!"

"Tough, Katherine. Look at it." Sue Ann pulled her hair out of her face. "Look at my face and choke on it. You ain't ever getting me outta this house. I'm a reminder of Leonard's dirty deeds and recklessness."

"You're the one to correct my daddy's sins, Sue Ann?" Charlie chewed. "God help us all."

Fiona snickered.

"I'm sick of you guys looking down on me!" Sue Ann shoved her plate. "The damn hunting dogs get more respect than me."

"That's because *they* know how to act," Katherine snapped. "Look at yourself, Sue Ann. You are a disgrace and getting worse every day. An embarrassment to the Bernstein name."

Sue Ann rolled her eyes.

"We wanna get close to you, but you make it so darn hard. Charlie and I have been more than patient with your antics."

"I want a drink, Katherine." Sue Ann clenched her teeth. "I don't wanna hear this fake song and dance about you guys caring about me because you don't."

Charlie sipped wine. "If we didn't, would you be here? No. What more do you want from us, Sue Ann? You're tired of being looked down upon? Well, I'm tired of having to feel guilty because I was born to privilege and you weren't. It's not my fault how your life turned out."

"I was born to privilege too!" She hit the table. "That's what you don't seem to get, Brother. Stop acting like you are doing me a favor when I'm just as much of a Bernstein as you. Leonard Bernstein was my father. I'm not some charity case, and you guys better start respecting me."

"Or what?" Charlie dabbed the corners of his mouth. "I'd love to know what you'd do if we don't?"

"You don't *deserve* respect, Sue Ann." Katherine shook her head. "You *earn* it and you haven't."

Something tumbled down the hall, followed by the sound of shattering glass.

"My Lord." Fiona touched her bosom.

"Ah!" Charlie banged the table. "Big Pearl!"

"Yeah, Big Pearl!" Sue Ann cackled. "Tear this whole damn place down!"

"We won't have a house left with him around," Charlie said. "Big Pearl, get in here!"

The big fella came in, huffing and puffing. "I'm sorry, Mr. Charlie. I'll fix it. I'll fix it!" Big Pearl bolted back out of the room, sweating.

"Jesus," Charlie said. "He spends more time repairing what he's broken than doing his job."

Fiona covered her grin.

"Big Pearl ain't the one breaking stuff in this house." Sue Ann snickered but Fiona could see her pain behind the smile. "Everything in it is already broken."

"I'm done." Charlie wiped his mouth, got up, and left.

Sue Ann smirked at Katherine, who left without another word.

Soon it was just Fiona and Sue Ann, practicing an awkward staring match.

"Are you all right, Miss Sue Ann?"

She dragged her fork through the steak juice on her plate. "Why do you care? The family sure don't."

"Your supper's getting cold. Is there anything else I can get you?"

"Yeah." Sue Ann dropped the fork. "How about a new life and a new family? Someone who cares about me?" Her eyes watered. "How about *that*?"

"If I may say so, I don't think that's your problem, ma'am."

"What are you talking about, girl?"

Fiona clasped her hands in front of her. "The problem doesn't seem to be them not loving you, but you not loving yourself. If you did that, you wouldn't care what anyone thought."

"What do you know?"

Fiona shrugged. "I know you'd be a lot prettier if you paid more attention to yourself. If you let people see you for who you really are and frankly Miss Sue Ann, this ain't you. And I know it ain't who you wanna be."

"You know so much, Fiona?" Sue Ann's forehead wrinkled. "After just *weeks*?"

"I knew you well the first time I laid eyes on you. How long you gonna hide? You got so much to offer, but you gotta realize it first."

"Instead of worrying about *me*, concentrate on what's going on between you and Charlie."

Fiona threw her shoulders back. "Excuse me?"

Sue Ann twiddled her fingers against the table. "I hope you're prepared for the storm coming your way, Fiona. When my brother gets a hold of you, and he will, you'll wish you never heard of Charlie Bernstein. Just you wait." She stood, shoving her chair against the table. "If you're as smart as you act like, you'd leave right now."

"I don't know what you talking about. There's nothing going on between me and Mr. Charlie, and there never will be."

"It's a big house, but you can't run from him forever. He's gonna get his way. He always does. I just hope you remember your own advice about loving yourself after he breaks your heart."

Sue Ann pranced out of the dining room.

CHAPTER SIX

Fiona sighed as she bumped into Charlie in the hallway that night. She knew her luck would soon run out, and he'd catch her alone again. Sue Ann was right. She couldn't run.

Fiona went to pass him like she normally did, but Charlie pushed her against the wall by the portrait of his father and blocked her by placing his hands on both sides of her.

So here it was. The catalyst of his game. Never had he been so bold, but she wasn't surprised he'd finally had enough.

"Do you enjoy torturing me?" His damp lips shook. "Enjoy playing this game?"

"Mr. Charlie, I'm not the one playing games." She tried to leave, but of course he didn't move. "You are my employer and I've repeatedly said I don't think we should do this."

"I don't care what you think."

"That's quite clear, Mr. Charlie."

"I... I can't do this anymore, Fiona." His forehead wrinkled. "Watch you prance around here in *my* house, calling the shots while I go crazy. Enough! I pay your salary, and *I* make the rules."

"Mr. Charlie, you're sounding more and more like a *massa* instead of a master of the house."

He swallowed, jaws flexing.

"You seem to think I'm your property, but that couldn't be farther from the truth."

"You sure are an uppity one, ain't you? A Negro maid who thinks she's better than me?"

"They say there's two kinds of men in this world, Mr. Charlie. But that's a lie because there's *one* kind. You're all alike no matter your color or station. Just want what you want when you want it, no matter how it affects someone else." She tried to move again, and this time he grabbed her and held her against the wall. "Mr. Charlie!"

"You're driving me crazy and it's unlike anything I've ever felt." His eyes dug into her soul. "Tonight during dinner, even when Sue Ann was throwing her usual fit, I wanted to kiss you. Heck, I wanted to do so much more and if they hadn't been in the room, I would've."

"Mr. Charlie, please—"

"I wanted to respect your feelings. I know this job is important to you." He squeezed her arms. "And I admire that, Fiona. You are such a courageous woman. Never have I seen that before. You came here on your own, not knowing anyone or anything. You just threw caution to the wind

and that's what *I've* always wanted to do."

She panted.

"Then you told me you'd been homeless. And I found you even more remarkable. And look at the West Pine thing. You're fighting to help them. Standing up for the cause with Greta Fay to keep those people in their homes and you don't have to give a damn about them." He chuckled. "You're putting your life on the line and you have no fear, Fiona. No fear." He grabbed her face with both hands, his weight crushing her as he pressed his smothering lips to hers.

"Mm, no!" She pushed him away and ran down the hall to her room and, just as she suspected, Charlie followed. "Please, Mr. Charlie." She tried to close her bedroom door, but he pushed it forward. "What do you *want*?"

"You." He sauntered inside, his gaze burrowing into her. "You're so worldly and charming. Even more than those high-society women I'm forced to take out for tea. They're so boring and predictable, and you're free and adventurous."

"Adventurous?" She backed up as he walked toward her. "Why would you say that? I've done nothing to give you that idea."

"Are you kidding?" He sweated. "Look at the way you fight me. No one has ever resisted me before in business or romance. But that's not all, Fiona. You're reminding me what it's like to be a man outside of the Bernstein name. I am so sick of this life!"

"Really?" She backed up to the bookshelf. "I bet you many people in this world wish they had a life like yours to be sick of. You don't even appreciate it."

"All the money in the world can't give me what you've given me, Fiona. The minute I saw you, I saw my freedom. Someone to rescue me from this world." He tugged at his tie. "You're just like me. You came here to escape your life and God sent you here so I could escape mine." He reached for her and she ran to the window.

"This is crazy, Charlie! God sent me here to do a job, nothing more. I'm not some savior."

"I've never felt this way about any other woman, and I've been with *many*. None of them have lit the fire inside me you have. You're my breath of fresh air, Fiona. I know my life seems perfect, but it's anything but and I get so tired of being seen as a name and not a *man*."

"Guess I can relate." She touched the window. "Because I get sick of being seen as a color and gender and not a person."

"I see you, Fiona." He grabbed her. "You're all I see!"

"Wait!"

He threw her on the bed, got on top of her, and washed her with his kisses.

"Charlie." She squirmed, pushing at his chest. "Charlie, stop!"

He leaned up, his lips puckered in mid-kiss.

"We can't do this." She tried to calm her breathing. "This isn't just some pastime for me. It's my job."

"You don't wanna be with me because I'm your boss? That makes no sense, Fiona. Me being your boss brings you security."

She held him back as he tried to kiss her again. "What if we have an affair and fall out? If you end up hating me and throw me out? I'll have nothing. My family depends on me, Charlie. I came here for a better *life*."

"Then let me give that to you!" He shook her. "Look around, Fiona. You couldn't get a life any better than the Bernstein name."

She lifted her head, squinting. "You mean the life you just said you wanted to run away from?"

"You said you read romances because it's your dream to have a man who would love you like no other. Well, he's here, Fiona. He's me."

"No." She shook her head. "The man I dream of is not you. He can't be you, Charlie! Please, get off me."

"I'd never force myself on you, Fiona. But I'm warning you, my desire is becoming an obsession."

"How is this different from all the other women you've chased? How do I know I'm not another conquest? The easiest one to go after, no doubt?"

"It's not whether you believe it. It's whether you *want* to." He kissed her again and at first her breath stopped as if she'd black out, but then the more they held the passion, the easier it became for her to breathe.

She didn't know what came over her, but she shoved her fingers into his silky waves and melted within the heat of his craving for her. This was Fiona's first kiss and something told her that no matter how long she lived, no man would ever make her feel as good as she felt at this moment.

Charlie ripped his lips away, panting. "We must stop or I won't be able to."

She realized he was asking her permission and despite her just telling him why he wasn't good for her, she couldn't form the words to push him away.

"Please, don't do this to me." He breathed as he kissed down her lacey nightgown. "Don't tease me, Fiona."

"What?" The breath in her chest was so tight it felt like bricks pushing against her. "What are you talking about?"

"Don't pretend this is happening..." He squeezed her tingling breasts through the thin material. "And then stop me when I get going because it'll kill me, Fiona. It will *kill* me."

"Did I say anything about stopping?" She couldn't believe the whorish words that floated from her mouth. Her Mama and Papa would've slapped her if they'd seen her now. She was doing exactly what the women in her family had warned her not to do; fall for the white man's charming tongue and become another Negro concubine.

Fiona had agreed with all that until this moment. Because while her sister and mother were warning her against falling for Charlie, they forgot to warn her about how good his kisses would feel. Or how smoldering hot her skin would be when he touched her. How every time his fingertips tickled her skin, she'd break out in goosebumps.

No, they hadn't told her none of that.

Charlie's kisses were unlike anything she'd ever felt. Like the chocolate cake Mama brought home sometimes. Her mother worked for a white lady in Braesville. She cleaned her house, and the lady was a baker and she'd give Fiona's mother leftover cakes and pies. Fiona loved chocolate cake, and that's exactly what Charlie's kisses felt like, swallowing the first bite of chocolate cake.

With his lips plastered over hers and moaning, he grabbed at her gown and hiked it up.

Her instinct was to tell him no. It was the lady in her, but this was the right time. Here and now.

Kissing her breasts through her gown, he fumbled with her lacey drawers. "Ah." He sighed with relief as he ripped them off of her as if he was about to take his first drink of water after being stuck in the desert for weeks.

Rocking underneath him, Fiona grabbed his large shoulders, looking at the lantern above them.

This wasn't like in the romance books she'd read. Where the first time was carefully planned out by the hero. Shoot, this wasn't even what Fiona had thought her first time would be like. But that was life.

Charlie didn't have to wine and dine her. He didn't have to give her gifts or whisper sweet nothings. His passion, his desire, came from how he kissed her. His touch. The way his voice growled from a need to hold her when he said her name.

"Oh, I've dreamed of this moment since I first saw you in the garden." He pulled down his trousers, rubbing his soft sideburns against her face. "This is what I wanted to do to you, then."

"Show me." She squeezed his shoulders from anticipation *and* fear. "I've wanted this too. I don't know what power you have over me, Charlie. You make me wanna run to trouble instead of away from it."

"We'll be trouble together, Fiona. Look into my eyes."

She did, and they sang a song of compassion and fascination.

"Do you know what 'fucking' is?"

She batted her eyes. "It's not a word most ladies would admit to knowing but I have a father and uncles so, yes."

"That's what I wanna do to you now. I wanna fuck you, Fiona. Not make love to you. Fuck you. Is that okay?"

"I'm laying here with my legs wrapped around you and your hand on my crotch. Aren't we beyond formalities?"

Snickering, Charlie yanked down his trousers. There was no exploring each other's bodies or painting each other with timid kisses. No this was the intense need to let something out. Something they couldn't control because their bodies had long ago decided this would happen.

Charlie lifted her leg and with his waistcoat and shirt still neat and hair perfect as if he'd

just combed it, he entered her.

Fiona gasped as his thickness widened her walls.

Grabbing her head, he rocked gently at first then like a storm, each level of movement became more treacherous and she had to hold on to him for fear of falling off the bed.

Grunting and wincing, Charlie held her arms down as he pounded her with his magnificent cock. He forced sounds out of Fiona she never knew existed. Opened her up inside and out and she knew she could never go back to how things were before.

"Ooh." He squeezed his eyes shut. "Oh."

She kept her eyes open. She wasn't sure if that was normal or not but she loved looking at the pleasure she brought him. His face couldn't lie. He looked like Sue Ann when she saw liquor: *alive*.

She wanted to moan, but it felt so unnatural. She used the time to explore him. It didn't matter he was still fully dressed from the top. She let her hands roam, feeling his muscles through layers of clothing.

It confused her how men could feel so soft and hard at the same time. Charlie's skin was like elastic. She'd touch it and it would bounce back into place.

She loved it when he'd bend his head down mid-thrust so she could smell the bear grease in his hair. She caressed his back and then brought her hands to his naked romp, squeezing as he drilled deeper inside of her.

"Yes, oh!" He sweated more than Big Pearl out in the yard.

As Charlie stroked, every nerve in Fiona's body stood at attention. His thrusts forced moans and screams that she tried so hard to stifle. Thank goodness the servant's quarters was way across the mansion from Katherine. But Miss Mildred probably heard.

Hell, it felt so good Fiona didn't even care. The more he fucked her, the more intense that ball of fire inside of her felt. She was so moist and sticky, the air around them smelling like a sandwich made from private parts. Manly, feminine, natural.

Fiona wrapped her arms around his shoulders and tightened her legs against his waist as that snowball of nerves got bigger and bigger and bigger until Charlie gave her that next poke and she crumbled.

"Ah!"

Whatever it was, came fast. Too fast and there was a reason for it because another one brewed.

Charlie kept thrusting as she dug her fingers into the fine silk of his shirt. "Come again," he whispered. "I'm gonna make you come again!"

So she'd just come? That fast? The way her sister had described it, she thought it would've taken forever, but it shot out of Fiona like a bullet. Maybe that's what happened when your body wanted someone as much as she wanted Charlie.

He grabbed her gown by the lace lining on the bosom and ripped it halfway, freeing her breasts. He massaged them, gently, panting as he kept up his rhythm.

"Yes, Charlie." She laid back, enjoying his palms against her nipples. "That feels so good."

Then he did what she'd wanted him to do in her dreams. He sucked her breasts. Lightly at first then he went into frenzy as if he were milking her with his mouth.

He moaned and slurped, not even coming up for air.

Fiona looked at him as he sucked her breasts and fucked her. She couldn't believe this was finally happening. She was having sex and with Charlie Bernstein! One of the richest men ever born.

"Oh, yes." She stretched out her arms, feeling empowered. Here was this powerful businessman on top of her, writhing and she was in control because he wanted her so much he couldn't contain himself.

Fiona grabbed his face and covered his lips with a sloppy kiss, showing him who was boss. Despite how good his cock felt, she loved kissing him the most because she felt him tingling each time their lips touched.

It would hurt a bit, him stretching and moving inside of her. The foreign fullness in her mound. But the minute she showed pain either with a whimper or wince, Charlie was there, comforting her, kissing her.

Fiona's sexual confidence grew with each moment. She figured out he loved his neck sucked.

So she gave him more than he could handle, sucking that spot until it turned red.

Nothing compared to being this close to someone. Nothing more intimate than making love, fucking whatever you wanted to call it. Words didn't matter. What Fiona cared about was being in this man's arms and how her body reacted in harmony every time he touched her.

She came again. Again and again. She lost count. Didn't know if it was normal and didn't care. Maybe it was natural or maybe it was Charlie's expertise.

Fiona just embraced it. She didn't think about how she was supposed to act or what she needed to say. She closed her eyes and rode the waves of her feelings. Back and forth. Up and down until finally, with her urging, touching, and thrusting... Charlie came too.

CHAPTER SEVEN

Time flew fast in Charlie's arms and that's exactly where Fiona spent her time for the next month, wrapped up in Charlie's embrace. In his love. Every chance they got, they spent it together. Charlie insisted they not be so bold in front of the family and they certainly couldn't take their romance outside of the mansion walls, but they made every moment count.

Fiona learned about Charlie's home in the most interesting ways. He'd given her the grand tour of every nook and cranny. Of course, this comprised them both being naked and going crazy on each other.

They did it *everywhere*.

Closets. The stables. The washrooms. The garden. In the upstairs hallway when everyone had retired for the night. Even in the shed that Big Pearl hadn't even finished yet. Right there, Charlie had Fiona naked on the wood, giving it to her while she got splinters in her butt. And she wouldn't have it any other way.

They even did it in the back of the carriage when the coachman took them into town. Fiona's favorite spot was the cellar. It was on the ground level, so they had to descend all those creepy stairs, but once they got down there, nothing could stop them. And it wasn't just Charlie with the crazy sex drive, either. Sometimes Fiona didn't even know her own strength, and she'd learned the art of getting Charlie out of his clothes in record time.

It helped they were quiet lovers. Charlie barely made the peep of a mouse when he came and due to all this hiding, Fiona had learned to keep quiet as she got her pleasure, too.

Fiona had never been so consumed with another human. She breathed, ate, and dreamed about Charlie Bernstein and she couldn't keep her hands off him.

An innocent walk in the garden after dinner? That turned into a sweaty, skin-scratching romp behind the bushes.

Charlie peeping into her room to say goodnight? They ended up doing this thing he'd taught her called 69, and it was absolutely glorious.

And though she wasn't very experienced, she knew Charlie was the best lover she'd ever had. He molded her body like a sculpture. Made it his own personal canvas where he could do

what he wanted.

The only problem was, Fiona didn't wanna fall in love. She kept saying she wouldn't. Even

prayed to God to make sure she didn't. But by the time that month was over, she knew better. Charlie Bernstein was her man.

The love of her life.

Charlie stayed on Fiona's brain every minute of every day and he was on her mind when Big Pearl took her into town to get Charlie's favorite chicken seasoning for that night's dinner.

With all that smiling and giggling Fiona did, Big Pearl had to know something was going on between her and Charlie. She didn't care. It was Charlie, after all, who insisted they be discreet and she'd take him any way she could get him.

"Miss Fiona, you sho' smiley today." Big Pearl handled the reins right beside her, with the carriage leaning to one side because of his weight.

"Careful, Big Pearl." Holding her sun umbrella, Fiona checked the wheel on her side. "You sure we ain't gonna tip over?"

"Naw. This carriage is bigger than ours at home and I get in it with my whole family."

"Just slow down a bit, will ya'?" Fiona wobbled. "I don't wanna end up a pancake in the middle of the road."

Big Pearl had a hearty laugh. "You sho is funny, Miss Fiona. The stuff you be saying. What you gotta get at the grocery again?"

"Some of that garlic seasoning Charlie like." She curled up her nose. "Lord knows why. It stinks up the house and be on his breath for days."

"Yeah, Mr. Charlie like garlic, don't he?"

"I appreciate you taking me to town, Big Pearl. I can't drive a carriage."

"It's no problem, Miss Fiona. I was glad to do it." His pearly teeth gleamed in the sun. "Uh, you like working for Mr. Charlie, huh? You two seem to get on well."

She looked at him from the corners of her eyes. "That's supposed to mean something, Peter?"

"Oh, no." He shook his head, that raggedy cowboy hat shaking. "I just meant that you two seem kinda close. Now it ain't my business. Just saying what I seen."

"Mr. Charlie is my employer, Big Pearl." She fixed the skirt of her dress. "That's all."

"I wasn't implying anything, Miss Fiona. I know you a decent lady."

"Uh-huh."

"Speaking of which, old Eddie still wanna come a-calling if you interested. Man, he gone

crazy over you." He guffawed, shaking the carriage more than the horses did. "He *love* him some Fiona Acres."

"I appreciate your cousin's interest, Big Pearl, but I ain't looking for no husband."

He stuck his lips out. "Why not? Eddie a good guy, and the women love him. Think he the most handsomest man some do. He got that... what you call it?"

"Charisma?"

"Yeah that!" Big Pearl snapped his fingers. "Every single Negro woman I know wanna marry him. Or is that the problem?"

"I ain't say he ain't good-looking and from what I've seen, he'd make a fine good husband. Just not for me." She looked ahead. "Nothing personal."

"But you gotta think about it, Miss Fiona. You twenty-one. You gonna be a spinster in a few years. Don't you want marriage and kids?"

"Of course." She squeezed the umbrella shaft. "But I got time. I wanna be in love with my husband."

"That sounds good, but it ain't realistic. See, a lot of folks 'round here get married because it's the best thing for them. That's what you do in Clear Creek County." He nodded. "You get you a little pretty wife or hardworking husband, settle down, have kids and die."

She laughed. "Well, that sums up a life in about five seconds, don't it, Big Pearl? What about you and Cindy? Don't you love her?"

"Of course." He grimaced. "Cindy is my heart and Little Pearl mean the world to me. But shoot, I ain't foolin' myself. Cindy didn't love me at first." He raised his bushy eyebrows. "Between you and me, I knocked Cindy up befo' marriage."

She gasped. "Big Pearl, you didn't!"

"I did but the family don't know she was already pregnant by the nuptials." He batted his eyes. "Ain't proud of it, but thangs happen in the heat of passion. My point is, Cindy ain't love me at first. She married me because it was the right thing to do. She love me now though." He smiled.

"I'd expect any decent woman would marry if she fell pregnant, Big Pearl."

"So you would too?" He looked at her. "Marry if you got pregnant?"

"Of course. What decent woman would be pregnant and unmarried? But I don't plan on getting pregnant right now."

"You don't always plan these thangs, Miss Fiona. Weren't you just listening to the story I was telling you?"

She glared at him.

They got into town and it was like a whole different world. Fiona hadn't been to town much since she arrived. She had to get used to being around so many people again.

Town represented what she'd missed. Life.

Kids ran through people, throwing fruit at each other. Women in their common dresses and hats dashed down the sidewalks, jabbering with each other. Men moseyed through the crowd, walking in front of others and paying no mind.

"Good Lord," Big Pearl said. "Sho is busy today, ain't it?"

"Move it, boy!" An old white man in an apron grimaced at their carriage.

"Sorry, sir," Big Pearl said.

The man grumbled and went on his way.

"Look at the grocery mart." Fiona pointed a gloved finger. "Look at all them people, Big Pearl. We'll never get outta here. We colored. We gonna have to wait until all them folks get out the line. We could be here all day."

"Don't worry, Miss Fiona. We work for the Bernsteins." He winked. "That carries a lot of weight in this town."

Big Pearl was right. They got into the store and people parted like they were royalty. The store folks knew Big Pearl worked for Charlie and they let him and Fiona go right in, get what they needed and check out.

"See?" Big Pearl chuckled, patting his thick belly as they walked out of the market. "Told you we wouldn't have no problems."

"You was right." Fiona sashayed past a group of white men who stared at her with pure indecency on their minds. She'd have clutched her pearls if she wore any.

Big Pearl moved Fiona over to the other side so she didn't have to pass the men. "I'm sorry about that, Miss Fiona. Them lookin' at you that way."

"Thank you, Big Pearl." She touched her bonnet. "Seems like some things never change, huh? I thought Clear Creek County was so different from Braesville."

"Negro or not, them men should show you some respect." Big Pearl shuffled along in those

baggy, dusty suspenders. "They wouldn't dare look at a white lady like that."

Fiona brushed past people on the crowded sidewalk.

"Miss Fiona, would you like to have dinner with me and my family tonight? I told them so much about you. Plus, you and Greta Fay seem to get along well."

"Oh, I love Greta Fay. Admire her spunk." Fiona beamed. "I'm so impressed with all she's doing in the town to help black folks."

"She got some news on the West Pine thing, too."

"I'd love to come to dinner with your family. I'd like that very much."

He smiled, showing them teeth again.

"Uh, Eddie won't be there, will he?"

"*No.*" Big Pearl huffed. "Eddie won't be there."

She grinned. "Okay, I can't wait to come."

They got to the carriage.

"Let me take this and help you up." Big Pearl took the sack and placed his hands on Fiona's waist to hoist her up when a shiny black carriage stopped beside them.

"Oh, no." Big Pearl sighed.

"What?" Fiona checked out the carriage. "Man, that thing's fancy."

Two gorgeous Negro women with makeup as perfect as polished dolls, hats that looked like they cost a fortune, and silk, embroidered dresses even some white women couldn't afford, stuck their heads out of the carriage.

"*Hello,*" one said with a low and sexy drawl. "I'm Gladys. You Fiona, right?"

"Uh, yes." Fiona had to shake her head to stop from staring, but she'd never seen Negro women this put together before. "How do you know my name?"

"Never mind," Big Pearl said. "Gladys, Irma, why don't you two go on about yo' business?"

"No need to be like that, Big Pearl." Irma stuck out her juicy cleavage. "You know, the offer still stands for some company."

"Yeah, Big Pearl." Gladys played with her black ringlets. "We know Cindy can't be satisfying such a big, hungry man like you. But we can."

The women cackled.

"Yeah, we can satisfy you quite well." Irma blew him a kiss.

"Get gone." Big Pearl stuck out his chest. "Miss Fiona ain't got no business with the likes of you."

"Hold on, Big Pearl." Fiona nudged him in his stomach. "I can speak for myself."

"See there?" Irma batted her curvy lashes. "She's interested. You see these nice clothes and fancy jewels?" She pointed to her earrings. "You don't get that from cleaning houses."

"Nope." Gladys shook her head, her long black ringlets hanging over one shoulder. "Traveling and being treated like a queen, you sho don't get *that* from cleaning houses either."

Gladys sparkled every time she moved from all that jewelry.

"And we all know what you two do to get that treatment," Big Pearl said. "And it's nothing a decent woman like Miss Fiona would be interested in."

"Oh." Fiona sighed. She hadn't wanted to assume the pretty Negroes were soiled doves, but it was more than obvious. "Big Pearl's right. I can't see why you'd want anything to do with *me*."

"We work for Carl Lansing." Gladys had suggestive almond-shaped eyes that Fiona guessed made men go crazy. "It's a life a colored girl could only dream of."

"Don't matter how you get the money," Irma said. "It's what you do with it. The money we get from Carl got our family living good. Yeah, we take trips to New York, Texas, you name it."

"You been to New York?" Fiona asked. "I ain't been nowhere but Braesville and Clear Creek County."

Big Pearl groaned.

"You're a pretty woman, Fiona." Irma bounced her cleavage. "You could be sitting here with us riding in a fancy carriage with men paying yo' way. Or you can keep cleaning houses for Charlie Bernstein." A breeze blew at the feather in Irma's hair. "It's your choice."

"If you ever get tired of *being* tired, Fiona..." Gladys grinned. "Come see Carl. He'll introduce you to a whole other world. If you ain't afraid to see it. Let's go!" she shouted to the coachman. "Bye, Fiona." Gladys waved at Big Pearl. "Bye, Peter Pearl."

"Yes." Irma blew him a kiss. "Bye Peter. Tell Cindy we said hello."

The women cackled as the carriage carried on.

"Come on, Miss Fiona. Let me help you." Big Pearl helped her into the carriage and plopped into the driver's seat, rocking the entire vehicle. "You ready?"

"Yep." Fiona laid the grocery sack in her lap.

"Okay, let's go." Big Pearl took the reins. "Hey, look. There's Mr. Charlie."

Sure enough, there was Charlie laughing and blushing, but Fiona didn't focus on *him* as much as she did the beautiful white black-haired lady, holding Charlie's hand.

Charlie and the woman walked snuggled up together. He'd whisper in her ear and she'd lower her sun umbrella enough to hear whatever sweet-nothing he'd said. Medium-height, the woman had a petite frame but luscious bosom and she seemed to take pride in showing it off.

"Maybe we should go say hello," Big Pearl said.

Fiona heard Big Pearl say something, but it didn't register. She just kept staring at Charlie and how happy and attentive he was to this gushing woman. How he held her hand and seemed to walk with pride because she was on his arm.

All the things he never did when he was with Fiona.

"Miss Fiona?" Big Pearl patted her hand. "Are you all right? You look piqued."

She shook from her thoughts. "I'm fine. Let's just go on."

"You don't wanna say hello to Mr. Charlie?"

Charlie and the woman stopped at the flower stand and he got her a bouquet. The woman's pale face lit up with fascination.

"He looks awful busy," Fiona said. "Um, we don't wanna disturb him and I need to get this seasoning back to the cook."

Big Pearl's forehead wrinkled in confusion. "Okay." He navigated the carriage, but the square was so crowded and Charlie was so fixated on the woman he was with, he didn't see Fiona and Big Pearl passing.

"Big Pearl?"

"Hmm?"

Fiona looked back once they got a safe distance away from Charlie and the woman. "Who was that woman with Charlie?"

"Oh, that's Miss Jane Locke. Mr. Charlie's been courting her off and on. I think she's been out of town."

"She's a Locke?" Fiona exhaled. "What a surprise."

"They sure make a fetching couple, huh? Don't you think they look good together, Miss Fiona?"

"Yeah." She looked ahead, batting away tears. "They look *great.*"

CHAPTER EIGHT

Fiona sprayed the flowers in the garden that evening, not able to get Charlie and Jane out of her head. What she'd hoped wouldn't happen, happened. She'd not only fallen for Charlie Bernstein, but just as she predicted, he broke her heart.

Fiona sniffled, caressing petals of various colors.

She just didn't think it would happen so fast. How could she be such a fool to think Charlie cared about her? She was just something to play with until his beloved Jane got back. Why would he want a maid when he could be with a rich and desirable woman like Jane Locke?

Overwhelmed with emotion, she broke into tears. She didn't wanna give Charlie the satisfaction of crying about him, but this was the first time a man had ever broken her heart. And probably the last time she'd let a man get so close to it.

The elaborate wooden door with the stained glass opened, and Charlie strutted into the garden with that sexy smile.

Fiona turned away so he couldn't see her tears.

"There you are." He hopped up to her and hugged her from behind. "I missed you so much. I couldn't get you off my mind all day. These are for you." He held the roses in front of her. "Sorry, but they don't make flowers as beautiful as you."

Fiona whisked around and walked past him so fast, the hem of her dress rose.

"Fiona?" Charlie grabbed her before she could go back inside. "What's the matter?"

"Let me go." She didn't push at him out of respect because he was still her boss, but it took every amount of strength she owned not to shove those roses down his throat. "Keep your roses, sir. I have no use for them."

"Wait, a minute." He jumped in front of her. "I don't understand. Did I do something? This morning you were fine and now you're so mad your ears are steaming."

"I'm not mad." She closed her eyes. "I'm hurt."

"Fiona." He straightened his posture. "I demand you tell me what's wrong."

"You don't wanna know what I have to say, sir." She walked to the hedges, hugging herself.

"I brought you these beautiful flowers and you treat me this way?" He flung her around. "You damn well better tell me why."

Another tear fell as she looked into his fascinating eyes. "Why don't you give them to Jane

Locke? They suit her better."

"Jesus." He dropped his shoulders and shook his head. "You saw me with Jane?"

"Big Pearl took me into town to get your garlic seasoning." She chuckled. "Imagine my surprise when I saw you walking around the square with the pretty raven-haired Jane Locke." She stuck her chin in the air. "Jane's a lovely name. A name of privilege."

"She means nothing to me."

"Oh, you looked like she meant a lot, sir."

"That was for show. Fiona, you know how this goes. I'm a Bernstein and she's a Locke. We're the two most prominent families in Clear Creek County. People expect us to be together."

"You don't have to explain yourself to me. I'm just the maid, after all."

"You stop it." He grabbed her arm. "You know you will never be just the maid to me."

"Then what am I?"

"You're the woman I love!" He waved the roses. "The woman I want to spend the rest of my life with."

"The woman you hide?" She wiped tears. "The woman you use for sex?"

"That's not true, and you know it." He unbuttoned his jacket, revealing his waistcoat. "Fiona, you do not know the pressure I'm under. I'm expected to get married and settle down. Have heirs—"

"Wait. Are you saying you're gonna *marry* her? Charlie, you can't be saying that!"

"I don't *want* to." Spit flew out his mouth. "But when you come from a place of privilege. There are certain rules."

"Your behavior is atrocious, sir! You treat women like horses. You get tired of one and you put it down to get another."

He groaned, looking down at the grass.

"You say you don't care about Jane, but does she love *you*?" Fiona crossed her arms. "I bet she does and you don't care! Just like you don't care how I feel—"

He grabbed her and smashed his lips over hers. For a second, Fiona forget her anger and

relinquished control to her body, but remembering how dangerous it would be to let him think everything was okay, she pushed him away.

"No." She wiped off his kiss. "Don't bury this behind your kiss or your sweet touch. You don't understand how much you've hurt me."

"Fiona." He pulled her to him again. "I love you with every breath. You're the reason my heart beats. I've learned so much about myself since you got here and I wanna keep learning with you by my side."

"I've learned a lot too. That I'm not as smart as I thought I was. I came here saying I wouldn't let anything stop me from my mission but I fell for you, Charlie. I did the one thing I told myself I wouldn't do." She sniffled. "I knew you were a charmer. A man blessed with a silver tongue that could drop any woman to her knees, and I fell for every line you told me."

"It wasn't a line!" He dropped the roses. "Damn it, I've never felt for anyone what I feel for you, Fiona. When we make love, can't you feel it? Damn it, woman, it's like our bodies were meant for each other. When I'm inside you..." He touched her cheek. "I feel like a man reborn. Like I'm being baptized or something. With you, I've found my purpose. Jane means nothing to me at all. Nothing."

"Do you expect things with me to continue?"

"Yes." He squeezed her cheek. "Because I can't go a minute without kissing you or holding you. It damn well better continue, Fiona."

"Are you going to force me to be with you?" She stood erect. "Is that what's happening?"

"No." He stood back. "Of course not, but surely your feelings haven't changed in a matter of hours. You're just upset. Take some time and think about this and you'll see why Jane is a necessary evil."

She wandered to the table and turned back around to face him. "If it's truly my choice, then my answer is no."

He squinted. "No to what?"

"To being with you." She clenched her hands. "I won't be your Negro concubine, Charlie. I won't let you climb into my bed at night, give me some gifts, then walk around town with Miss Jane Locke. No."

He hurried to her. "Fiona—"

"I've already sacrificed my dignity and I won't sacrifice anything else for you, Charlie Bernstein. I knew you'd hurt me." The tears fell heavier. "I knew it, but being with you felt so right I didn't care."

"Fiona, please." His eyes watered. "Please, just calm down. Don't hurt me like this."

"Hurt *you*? All those promises you made were just to get me in your bed."

"No, no, no!" He hugged her. "I care about you, Fiona. You gotta know that. Nothing I said to you was a lie. Please tell me you know that—"

"You took my virginity!" She pushed him off of her. "I wasted it on you!"

"Don't say that." He wept. "Fiona, I swear on everything I love you."

"I gave you a part of myself I can never get back. I wasted my heart and love on you." She tried to walk away, and he seized her.

"It wasn't a waste! I love you, but you damn well know we can't be together!" He let her go. "Not out there at least. Not in society."

"Society may not understand it but should we care?" She grabbed his waistcoat. "Charlie, if you love me, that's all that matters. That's all that matters!" She pushed her head into his chest. "Please, fight for me, Charlie. Show me you'll do anything to be with me. I need that."

"Listen." He patted her hair bun, his voice muffled with despair. "No matter what happens from this point on, whether I marry Jane and have children, I will *always* love you, Fiona. She will never, ever take your place."

"So you won't make a stand? You're not man enough to admit you're in love with your black maid?"

"It's not *about* you."

"Yes it is. It's about my status, my lack of education, my color. That's all it's about!"

"Lack of education? Don't make me laugh. You might not have gone to some fancy school but you're more worldly and intelligent than Jane Locke will ever be." He clenched her hands. "Say what you want about me but I will not let you say these awful things about yourself, Fiona. You measure up to anyone and don't let anyone say otherwise."

"I'm so worthy of you, huh? I'm not sure that's a compliment anymore."

His shoulders slumped. "Maybe it's not."

"It's over, Charlie."

"No." He blinked, his face wrinkling. "No, it's not. It never will be, Fiona."

"You said you'd respect my choice."

"Don't do this!"

"From now on I am your maid and nothing else. Never touch me again, do you understand?

If you do, I swear I'll leave."

"You're miles from home, and you have nowhere to go. You forgot you need this job to help your family?"

"I don't *need* this job, Charlie." She wiggled her neck. "Contrary to popular belief, I can find another job in Clear Creek County."

"Where? You don't even know anyone else here."

"Carl Lansing." She lifted her chin. "He seems interested in me working for him."

"Come on, Fiona." He grimaced. "Really? Do you know what Carl does? He has his hand in every ounce of dirt in this town. Racketeering, robbery, blackmail, extortion, kidnapping, and yes, prostitution. You telling me you'd rather work for a man like that than to be with me?"

"I'm saying you ain't the only game in town. I mean it, Charlie." She raised her eyebrows. "If you lay a hand on me, I'm gone."

"*Why*?" His entire body quivered. "Why are you *doing* this?"

"I thought you were a real man, Charlie. The man I'd read about in all those romance books. But you're not a man at all. Letting you kiss me and hold me was a mistake and I won't be making it again anytime soon."

"Fiona." He grabbed her as she passed him but let her go when he saw the look in her eyes. "This doesn't have to end. We can be together in secret. Nothing has to change."

"Me sneaking around like your sex slave? Who benefits from that but you? Now if you'll excuse me, Mr. Charlie, I have to continue my work."

"Fiona!"

She reached the patio door. "And I'm going to dinner at Big Pearl's tonight so if you need something, you'll have to ask someone else."

"Fiona, please!" He ran after her. "Fiona!"

She went inside and closed the door in his face.

CHAPTER NINE

Big Pearl's family welcomed Fiona to the dinner table with open arms. Eula even hugged her and dished up a hearty plate of venison, beans and biscuits. Meeting the Wills' had been the only resemblance of family Fiona had experienced since coming to Clear Creek County.

Fiona had only spent a few minutes with the Wills family and found them all a hoot in their own way. Big Pearl's little brother, Irwin, was the sarcastic one. Always had to put his opinion in and pouted more like a child instead of acting like the 20-something year-old man he was.

Fiona had clicked with Greta Fay right after meeting her a few weeks earlier. She was around Fiona's age but had the maturity of someone twice as old. An attractive, vibrant woman, Greta Fay's kindness shined as much as her smile.

Big Pearl's wife Cindy was around 20 and a thick, yellow-skinned woman with big fluffy hair like a sheep's behind. She struggled to nurse the chunky little Eula-Pearl AKA Little Pearl, a fat-armed, little yellow piglet who looked like she'd end up as big as both her parents in a few years. The cutest little thing Fiona had ever seen.

Big Pearl's parents, Archie and Eula, reminded Fiona of *her* parents; kind, big-hearted and all about family.

Fiona settled in just fine. The food was great, the company entertaining and best of all, she could forget about Charlie and Jane.

At least for a little while.

"Big Pearl, you and Cindy sure make pretty babies." Fiona ate some of her biscuit. "I reckon Little Pearl gonna have a brother or sister soon."

"Well..." Cindy tussled with the big, fussy baby. "We want one, so as soon as the Lord makes it happen, we are ready."

"Uh-uh." Archie chomped on beans. "Big Pearl need to get a job first."

Big Pearl smacked his lips. "Working for Charlie Bernstein ain't a job?"

"You just buildin' a shed," Archie said. "You need a long-term job before you start talkin' about mo' babies."

"Your father's right, Big Pearl." Eula sopped up bean juice with her biscuit. "You need to be

prepared if you bringing mo' chirren into this house."

"I'd had a good job if it weren't for Greta Fay."

Greta Fay sat back, sighing. "This again. Big Pearl, if you was such an asset, they wouldn't have fired you from the ranch."

"Y'all stop all that fussin'," Eula said. "We got company. Fiona, how do you like working for Charlie Bernstein?"

She grimaced, wriggling in her chair. "It's all right, I reckon. The pay is good."

Irwin muttered beside Fiona, "Stealing all our jobs."

"I'm sorry, Irwin." Fiona sipped apple cider. "What did you say?"

"Nothing," Archie said. "As always."

The family chuckled.

"Go on, please," Fiona said. "It's your house, so you have a right to speak your mind."

"I said why all you Braesville niggers coming to Clear Creek County and taking all *our* jobs?"

"*Boy*," Archie grumbled as he chewed. "Fiona, ignore him."

"It's fine, Mr. Wills. Is that uh, how a lot of the Negroes here see it? Us coming and taking jobs?" Fiona looked around the table, getting varying expressions. "I see."

"I don't feel that way." Archie swallowed. "We all colored. We can't get mad at y'all for

wanting the same thing we want."

"Yeah, but we ain't going to their town, Papa." Irwin chomped meat. "It's a difference and I bet if we was doing it they'd feel the same."

"Maybe some would." Fiona shrugged. "But not me. I'm like Mr. Wills. I want all Negroes to have a shot at a decent job. Truth is, it's even harder for Negro women than it is men. We don't have *that* conversation enough."

"She's right," Greta Fay said. "Men can get labor jobs and work places we can't. With us, it's only being a maid, nanny, even the midwife jobs are hard to get."

"Yeah, if it wasn't for Mr. Charlie I don't know where I'd be." Fiona cut into her meat. "Might be workin' for Carl Lansing or something."

"Naw." Archie grimaced. "No, sweetheart, you don't wanna do *that*."

"No, honey," Eula said. "Working for Carl Lansing is beneath you."

"Maybe, but I can't lie and say I'm not curious about the things that life can get you. I'm a

decent woman, of course. But I seen them pretty Negro women and started dreaming, is all."

"We ran into Gladys and Irma in the square today." Big Pearl chewed. "Miss Fiona done had

stars in her eyes ever since."

"Oh, yeah, they be so pretty for sure." Greta Fay nodded. "Look like shiny brown porcelain dolls sitting up there in them silk dresses, shawls, and pearls. But what they do to get it ain't nothing pretty. That's for sure."

"I'd never do nothing like *that*." Fiona batted her eyes. "But they travel and get treated like queens. It's obvious why some choose to do that over cleaning."

"Cleaning is honest work," Eula said. "You can look at yourself in the mirror when you get done every night."

Greta Fay chewed. "Gladys is Cindy's cousin."

"Yeah, but we don't claim her." Cindy wiped Little Pearl's mouth. "Gladys something else. I think she'd sleep with her own daddy if he paid her."

"*Cindy*," Eula shrieked. "Girl, hush your mouth! We won't have that heathenish talk around here. Ain't nobody sleepin' with nobody's daddy. Good Lord."

Fiona and Greta Fay grinned.

"Gladys' daddy is Cindy's uncle." Greta Fay drank from her mug. "He a preacher."

Fiona gaped. "Gladys' daddy is a preacher? I bet that makes interesting conversation at her family's house during dinner."

"Gladys tries to give me money for the baby." Cindy laid Little Pearl over her shoulder and patted her little wiggling romp. "But I told her I'd rather my baby eat grass than take money from her."

"She *will* be eating grass if Big Pearl don't find a steady job." Irwin laughed.

Big Pearl threw a biscuit at him.

Irwin proudly took a big bite out of it.

Eula chuckled. "Have mercy. Archie, do something with yo' kids."

"Oh?" He sipped, looking at his wife next to him. "They good and they yo' kids. They cut up and they mine?"

Fiona laughed, covering her mouth.

"Cindy just talking," Irwin said. "She know she'd take that money from Gladys in a heartbeat if it meant Little Pearl being okay."

"I wouldn't want to," Cindy snapped. "Yeah, I would, but that's blood money. Carl Lansing's

the devil and slicker than a snake."

"He should be ashamed of himself." Greta Fay drank. "He like a lion ready to pounce. Have his folks waiting in town when the carriages with the Negro women come. But he don't do that when the white women move to town."

"Yeah." Fiona nodded. "Yeah, he had them three fools waiting for me. Kit somebody."

"Ugh, Kit Adams." Greta Fay turned up her nose. "I can't stand him. He's a leech. Just hanging on Carl so he stay relevant. Ain't got nothing else going for him. Carl's full of it, though. He wanna act like he doing Negro women a favor, but just using them is all."

"And parading them women around ain't even half of what he do." Archie gestured to Fiona. "Just stay away from him. Once you get involved with a man like him, there's no turning back."

"Okay, enough about Carl." Greta Fay cleared her throat. "I got some big news to share about the West Pine takeover."

Archie set his drink down, wide-eyed. "Well, spill it, girl."

"I found out who's involved." Greta Fay chewed. "Wilber Haynes."

Eula gaped. "Wilber Haynes?"

"Who is Wilber Haynes?" Fiona asked.

"Oh, Mr. Wilber is big time." Big Pearl whistled. "He's an investment banker."

"What is an investment banker?" Fiona asked.

Irwin huffed. "Haynes makes tons of money selling companies for a commission. He ain't as rich as the Lockes or Bernsteins, but he's up there. He's known all over California."

"So Haynes is trying to buy West Pine?" Eula grimaced. "And put up hotels?"

"Uh-huh." Archie nodded. "Sounds like something Haynes would do."

"He's just a partner," Greta Fay said. "He's working with someone else, but I couldn't find out who it is."

"Damn, girl." Cindy rocked Little Pearl. "Where you gettin' this stuff?"

"The grapevine." Greta Fay smiled. "Where else?"

"It's gotta be a Bernstein or a Locke he's working with," Irwin said. "Ain't nobody else around here got that kind of money."

"No, it's definitely not a Bernstein." Fiona shook her head. "I talked to Charlie about this and he was very concerned, as if he'd never heard of it before."

"Wait," Irwin said. "You went running your mouth to Charlie Bernstein? Girl, you crazy?"

"I wanted to help you and everyone else in the neighborhood not lose their homes, so I'd think you'd be grateful."

"Back off, Irwin," Big Pearl said. "Miss Fiona is just trying to help. Mr. Charlie's nice with her, so he listens to her more than the other servants."

Irwin looked Fiona up and down. "I bet he does."

"Irwin." Archie raised an eyebrow. "Next time you wanna say something smart, just stick that fork right down your throat."

"It has to be a Locke working with Haynes then," Cindy said. "It'll come to the light soon enough."

Irwin muttered, "I still think it's a Bernstein."

"If Charlie knew the person doing this, he'd step in and stop it," Fiona said. "He doesn't want anyone losing their homes. It's shameful."

"With all due respect Fiona...." Irwin bit into his meat. "You can have your theory and I'll have *mine*."

CHAPTER TEN

Another week flew by in Charlie Bernstein's household and though it hadn't been easy, Fiona did a pretty good job of staying away from him. Oh, he'd try his hardest to talk to her: corner her in the hall, rushing into a room before she could leave, following her around while she worked. But Fiona held her ground.

Keeping her distance from Charlie was like pushing a knife into her heart. She missed his kisses, and the way his touch set her entire body on edge. She kept thinking about the first time they made love and every time she did, she got wet as if Charlie was inside her again.

She prayed just to get through the day. To combat the determined lust that built inside her. Even a few nights of her pleasuring herself between the sheets didn't comfort her. Nothing and no one would be enough but Charlie. Yet, she had to stay strong. God sure was testing her, though, in more ways than one. Because besides dealing with the agony of avoiding her true love, Miss Mildred informed the help that Charlie had invited Jane Locke, yes, the woman herself, to Charlie's for dinner that night.

And that's when the Lord's testing of Fiona took exceptional levels. It was one thing to avoid Charlie's sensual lips and begging eyes. But it was a whole different thing to stand in that dining room and watch Miss Jane Locke sit by Charlie and act like the woman of the house.

When not a moment went by that Fiona didn't wish she were Jane Locke.

"Katherine, your cook sure has outdone himself." Jane squealed, her bosom sitting up all plump and creamy, looking like she was about to bust out of her dress. "This haddock is so tender and I can taste the flavor of the coals with every bite. Can't you, darling?"

Fiona glanced at Charlie, who sat right beside Jane. He did a timid smile, doing his best not to look Fiona's way like the coward he was.

"I appreciate your hospitality." Jane giggled. "And may I say I love the new decorations. So modern and vibrant. Do you think so, Sue Ann?"

Sue Ann pulled a fish bone out of her mouth. "Yeah, I guess."

Fiona grinned.

Jane fidgeted, then plastered om that fake smile. "Uh, I can't wait for dessert. I bet it'll be just as marvelous as dinner is."

"Jane, would you like more wine?" Katherine asked.

"Oh, no, I'm fine."

"Honey, tell them about your trip to Los Angeles," Charlie said. "And the fascinating time you had with your cousins."

"Seeing the family was so refreshing." She sat back. "And I just laid in the sun and let it rain on my skin."

"You're definitely glowing." Katherine smiled.

"My cousin's wedding went fine, but Los Angeles sure is different." Jane gasped. "You should see how they are with their niggers."

Charlie cleared his throat, glancing at Fiona.

"In Los Angeles, they let their niggers sit at the table and eat with them," Jane shrieked. "Have you ever heard such a thing? And they treat 'em just like family too."

"I don't see nothing wrong with that." Charlie chewed. "I think it's great."

"Great?" Jane batted her eyes. "Charlie, surely you don't mean that. I'm worried that this practice will shift to Clear Creek County. The niggers are already getting too uppity for my liking."

Fiona straightened her shoulders, doing her best not to dump the entire table over on Jane.

"I mean, that Greta Fay girl is causing too much trouble." Jane's ringlets bounced every time she moved her head. "And she needs to be put in her place."

"Greta Fay?" Katherine sipped. "Is she the one going around for Negros' rights? I think it's a great idea. They're people like us, Jane."

"They are *not* like us!" Jane grabbed the table, her head bobbing. "That's the thinking I'm worried about, Katherine. That more people will think just because slavery is over, the Negro deserves everything the white man has created. No. And Greta Fay should be grateful for what she has. Had she been born a little earlier, she'd have been a slave. She wouldn't want that, would she?"

Fiona exhaled.

"No, I like things how they are around here." Jane gestured to Fiona. "See? Like your gal. That's how niggers should be. She's respectful, quiet and knows her place."

Fiona squinted, holding her breath.

"Uh, maybe we should get started on dessert now," Charlie said. "Fiona, would you mind bringing whatever the cook has prepared for our dessert, please?"

"Whoops." Jane knocked her fork under the table. "I'm so clumsy. Gal?" She snapped her

fingers at Fiona. "Crawl under there and get my fork."

Fiona gaped.

Sue Ann chuckled at Fiona's expression.

"Can she hear?" Jane looked around at the others. "Gal, get my fork. I just dropped it. Didn't you see me? I'll need a new one."

"Uh, I'll get it." Charlie climbed under the table, bumping it left and right, then popped up with the fork. "Fiona, please bring another fork."

"What is this?" Jane grimaced. "Did you just climb under this table, Charlie? *She* was supposed to get the fork."

"What difference does it make?" Charlie passed Fiona the fork, apologizing with her eyes.

She rolled hers and headed toward the doorway.

"Hold it, gal." Jane said.

Fiona sighed as she turned around.

"Next time I tell you to do something, you best do it." Jane snickered. "After all, I might be lady of the house soon and you can best believe if I am things around here gonna change. Won't be no more *asking* niggers but telling. Do you hear me, gal?" Jane tightened her lips. "Answer me."

Fiona glanced at Charlie, who dropped his head in shame.

"Yes," Fiona said.

Jane squinted. "Yes... *what*?"

Fiona lifted her head. "Yes, ma'am."

"That's how you talk to me, gal." Jane took Charlie's hand. "And don't you forget it."

Fiona flounced out of the room with her face drenched in tears by the time she got into the kitchen.

"Girl, what's wrong with you?" Miss Mildred pulled the sparkling queen cakes out of the wood-burning stove. "We gotta get these cooling fast." She fanned them to hurry the process. "They took longer than the cook thought. I hope Miss Jane won't be upset."

Fiona crumbled in despair just hearing Jane's name.

"Fiona." Miss Mildred rushed to her. "What is the matter?"

"Fiona!" Charlie ran into the kitchen, beads of sweat gathering on his forehead. "Can I talk to you for a second?"

"No." Fiona dashed out of the kitchen and out into the garden, blinded by tears.

Charlie followed like the wind. "Fiona, wait."

"Leave me alone. I'm so humiliated."

"Why? Jane's the one who acted like a nut!" He pointed to the house. "She should be ashamed of herself, and I don't condone it."

"Yet you said nothing to her." Fiona turned around. "You didn't stand up for me!"

"I did! I climbed underneath the table and got the fork—"

"Stop it, Charlie! You just sat there while she spoke to me like I'm some slave."

"What the hell do you want from me, Fiona?" He grabbed his waist. "What?"

"I want you to stand up for me and I..." She grabbed her head. "I—"

"*What?*"

"I wanna be Jane!" Her scream nearly broke the night sky. "I wanna be Jane, Charlie. That's what I want."

He looked at her, panting.

"I wanna be able to walk in the square with you and hold your hand." Her lips trembled. "I wanna go out and have men bow to me while I strut around like a princess." She touched her apron. "I wanna wear sparkling dresses, makeup, and have my hair in curls."

"You don't need any of that stuff and I don't care about it. That doesn't make a woman desirable, Fiona. You are more desirable to me than Jane Locke ever could be."

"But I want that life, Charlie." She sobbed. "I've always wanted that life. You think I *wanna* be a maid? I almost threw up watching Jane prance around like she's your wife. And is that gonna happen, Charlie? God, please, you can't marry her, you can't!"

"I told you that whatever happens between me and Jane, I will always love you."

"Darn it, stand up for me, Charlie!" She grabbed his jacket. "Why can't you go in there and tell Jane to stick it and tell everyone in there you love me? Don't you want the life I do? For us to be together without having to hide?"

"You know I do." His forehead wrinkled. "But that's not realistic, Fiona. Society will never
allow us to be together."

"Society, again?" She raised her arm. "Why do we have to care about *society*, Charlie?"

"Because we do! I didn't make the rules, Fiona. This is just how it is. We have places in
society and as much as I wish it wasn't like that, it is."

"You're ashamed of me. Damn you, Charlie!" She jumped on him, punching his chest. "You're ashamed of me!"

"I'm not!" He tussled with her, grabbing her flying arms. "Fiona, stop!"

"Liar!" She pushed him away. "You're ashamed of being seen with me. Stop blaming it on society!"

"I'm not ashamed of you, but you know nothing, *nothing* about my world. You think it's so easy for me, don't you? You just see a white man with money so I can't have problems, right?"

She sniffled, wiping her eyes.

"Everything is rosy for me, huh, Fiona? Well, that's crap. You don't know what I've been through and what I've gone through my whole life. My father never gave a damn about me. He treated me like another business he ran. Didn't show not one inch of affection!" He walked toward the bushes. "I don't think he ever told me he loved me, Fiona. Not once. Yeah, to the outside world, I have everything."

She turned to face him.

"But inside..." He touched his chest. "In my heart, it's been dead for years until you. All those other women were just shadows. Not even important enough for me to remember their faces. Just women I laid with to feel better. And I know it's not proper, but I was with a lot of women because being inside them was the only thing that made me happy." He twisted his face. "Not the money, Fiona. Not this house. I don't care about any of it. All I wanted was for my dad to say he loved me one time or put his arms around me once."

"Charlie, you grew up with more money than I could ever imagine. I'm sorry if I'm not crying about your plight."

He grimaced.

"You don't know a darn thing about a hard life, Charlie. You've had everything, everything. So don't expect pity from me about how Leonard Bernstein didn't hug you enough when he gave you everything else in the world."

He winced. "Oh, so my feelings aren't validated? Because I have money and because my struggles aren't the same as yours, they don't matter?"

"Stop trying to change the subject, Charlie." She approached him. "This is not about your

upbringing, but you not being man enough to tell society you're gonna love who you wanna love and then you expect me to sacrifice my dignity?" She scoffed. "You expect me to keep opening my legs to you while you parade around like a peacock with that disgusting Jane Locke? No. No! I meant what I said the last time, romance between us is dead unless you stand up for me the same way you would stand up for Jane!" She turned to leave but he grabbed her arm so hard she felt he'd yank it off. "Let me go."

"Where are you going?"

"I'm going inside to my quarters." She looked at the grass. Anything but him. "And I'm going to bed."

"Fiona, please." He let her go. "Try to see things from my eyes."

"No. You see them from *mine*." She straightened her spine. "Now go on back in there to your precious, lily-white Jane Locke with the fancy black curls and the shining dress. Play the part you were born to, Charlie. Kiss her hand and do all the things you should with your pretty white lady, but leave me alone. Because one thing I will not do is go back into that dining room and be treated like a piece of dirt. Not by Jane Locke, you, or anybody!" She pulled at her collar. "I may be the colored maid, but I have pride, Charlie. My parents raised me to never be ashamed of myself and I'm not, even if you are."

"I'm not ashamed of you! It has nothing to do with you, Fiona! Nothing!"

"I know it's *society*." She blew a quick breath. "You've shouted it enough, Charlie."

"That's because I want you to hear me. *Hear* the words I'm saying and understand them."

"Nothing wrong with my hearing. But I won't let a capable man blame his decisions or lack of them on society. Not a brilliant, sophisticated man like yourself, Charlie."

"I love you, Fiona." He dropped to his knees in front of her. "I'm professing my love to you right here and now. Why does anyone knowing matter?"

"Because it *matters*, Charlie! I don't wanna be your dirty little secret. You can't understand

that?"

"Please." He pulled her to him, crying into her skirt. "Forgive me, my love. Be understanding. Don't forsake me, please. I love you, Fiona. I love you!"

She wriggled from his whimpering.

"What can I do?" Tears blanketed his face. "*What*?"

"Go in there with the same amount of emotion you're showing now and tell them you love me." Fiona pointed to the house. "Tell Jane Locke to get out of your house and that you choose me. *Me*. The colored maid over her. Can you do that, Charlie?"

He sat on his knees, red-faced and sniveling.

"Yeah." Fiona shrugged. "That's what I thought."

They heard a commotion from inside.

Charlie got off the grass. "What is that?"

Fiona listened. "Is that Big Pearl yelling like that? My God he sounds mad."

"Charlie!" Jane's shouts shook the sky. "Charlie, help us! This nigger is crazy!"

Fiona and Charlie ran inside.

CHAPTER ELEVEN

Fiona gasped when she and Charlie made it back into the dining room.

Big Pearl stood in the doorway, shouting, with smoke shooting from his ears.

Katherine and Mildred yelled at him, demanding he calmed down.

Poor Jane was swatting at him with a chair like a wild animal was about to attack her despite Big Pearl not being anywhere near her.

Fiona know where Sue Ann had gone and didn't have time to ask.

"Oh, Charlie!" Jane dropped the chair and ran into Charlie's arms. "Thank God you're here. I was so scared. This big Negro's trying to kill us!"

Big Pearl tossed his fiery gaze at Charlie, and Fiona knew if she didn't step in the way, Charlie Bernstein would be toast.

"Big Pearl!" Fiona jumped in front of Charlie. "Don't you do anything that will get you locked up. What's wrong with you?"

"He came in here yelling for Charlie like a madman," Mildred said. "And scaring the heavens out of Miss Jane."

"Get out of here, Big Pearl." Katherine pointed. "Now!"

"No." He huffed and puffed, his eyes narrowing. "I'm not going anywhere until Mr. Charlie explains himself."

"Who the hell do you think you are, Big Pearl?" Charlie charged Big Pearl. "You've lost your mind yelling like this in my house, in front of these women. You're fired!"

"No, wait." Fiona grabbed Big Pearl's sweaty shirt. "Mr. Charlie, something's going on. Big Pearl wouldn't act like this for no reason—"

"I don't care what reason he's got." Charlie looked up at Big Pearl, seemingly not intimidated at all by the much larger and angrier man. "Big Pearl, you won't turn this place into a circus. Now you leave and never come back or I'll call the sheriff!"

"You so different, huh?" Big Pearl panted. "So different, Mr. Charlie? Least that's what I thought.

"What the...?" Charlie held his waist. "What the hell are you talking about?"

"Everybody knows half the Bernsteins are snakes in the grass. But I thought you was better.

Being so nice. Acting like you care about Negroes, but you worse than all of them, ain't you, Mr.

Charlie?"

"Quiet, Big Pearl!" Mildred approached him. "You can't talk to Mr. Charlie like that."

"Why?" Big Pearl kept his gaze on Charlie. "Because he this upstanding gentleman and I'm just a nigger working on his shed? All I want is for him to admit what he done and then I'll go. Are you man enough to do that, Mr. Charlie?"

"Boy..." Charlie squinted. "You're not gonna talk to me like this in my home."

"Big Pearl, please." Fiona grabbed his huge hand. "What's going on? You can't be acting like this."

"Why don't you tell her, Mr. Charlie?" Big Pearl asked. "Tell us *all* what's going on."

"Enough of this!" Charlie pointed to the floor, the tails of his jacket flying up. "Say what you have to say and then leave!'

"The West Pine deal." Big Pearl looked at Fiona. "Mr. Charlie is behind it. He's the one working with Wilber Haynes."

All the women gaped at Charlie.

"You're wrong, Big Pearl." Fiona stared at Charlie, hoping his face would give her a sign that this couldn't possibly be true. "Mr. Charlie wouldn't do anything like that. He's trying to help you."

Big Pearl shook his head. "Believe what you want Fiona, but I know the truth. Greta Fay told me with proof." He dug into his filthy pocket and pulled out a typed letter. "Look at it, Miss Fiona. Go on and read it."

She took it.

"What is that?" Charlie scowled. "I demand you tell me now!"

Fiona read through what appeared to be a contract confirming the building of a hotel in West Pine and signed by Wilber Haynes and Charlie Bernstein. "No." She reread it. "This can't be right, Big Pearl."

"It's the contract."

"Give me this." Charlie snatched the paper from Fiona and as he read it, his skin turned white as snow. "How did you get this? This is a copy of the contract."

"Oh my God." Fiona covered her mouth. "This is *true*?"

"What is going on here, Charlie?" Jane rushed to him. "What are they talking about? West

Pine?"

"How did you get this?" Charlie lowered the paper, quivering with rage. "Answer me, boy! How did Greta Fay get this?"

Big Pearl lifted his chin. "From Minnie Locke."

Jane grimaced. "Cousin Minnie? What does *she* have to do with this?"

"Nothing but she my sister's friend and she was nice enough to investigate for us. She talked to Garrett Associates, and they told her everything." Big Pearl smiled. "Guess it's good to have a Locke in your pocket, huh?"

"Charlie, answer me!" Fiona grabbed his arm. "Tell me this isn't true."

"Charlie?" Jane stood in front of him. "Looks like you got a lot of things to explain, like why this Negro has her hands on you like she's your lover and not the maid?"

"Charlie, answer me right now." Fiona fought tears. "If you did it at least be man enough to say it. Is this true?" She took the contract and shook it in his face. "Is this *true*?"

"Yes! Ah, ah, ah!" He banged himself in the head with his fists. "But let me explain!"

"Explain?" Fiona chuckled. "Explain? How are you gonna explain kicking all of those people out of their homes? You can't explain that!"

"Charlie?" Katherine approached him with her eyebrow raised. "You trying to take Big Pearl's home? The homes of all those people in West Pine?"

"No, you got it wrong! I didn't wanna take anyone's land, but it was the only place we could build the hotel. They rejected us for permits to build where we initially wanted to." He swallowed. "We knew we could build in West Pine with no fight, so we went after the land. But it was for the good of the community." He looked at Fiona as if she were the only one in the room. "This is going to bring more jobs to Clear Creek County and help the Negros. Fiona, you gotta look at the bigger picture. I didn't do this to hurt anyone. It's business."

Big Pearl closed his eyes and inhaled.

"So you couldn't build where you wanted to," Fiona said. "So you took the Negroes' land because you figured no one would care. But the people in that neighborhood care. The Negroes in this whole town care, and you didn't count on that, did you, Charlie? You thought that those hardworking and prideful colored folks were just gonna lay down and take any little scraps of money you give them but you were mistaken."

He tightened his lips.

"They turned out to be more than you can handle, so you got sneakier and nastier, trying to just straight kick them out. Families, Charlie. People with little children and babies. Hardworking folks who don't do nothing but mind their own business. These folks have fought harder than you ever could know, but that ain't enough." She stood up straight. "It ain't never enough, is it, Charlie? Because you people keep taking, and taking, and taking, and taking until it's nothing left to take! As if you haven't taken enough from colored folks already!"

Katherine covered her mouth.

"I have more respect for the racists who are honest. The ones like Miss Jane who tell us to our faces they don't like us and they don't want us around."

Jane looked away.

"I respect Jane a lot more than I respect you, Charlie." Fiona fought tears. "You pretend to care about us but then stab us in the back, the same way white people did the natives. No more!" Fiona swatted air. "We're not taking this anymore, Charlie! You are *not* getting that land. I don't care if we got to fight until we all die, you will *never* get West Pine."

"Fiona—"

"Don't touch me." She swatted his hand away from her. "You are the most disgusting, pathetic excuse for a man that's ever been born, and I curse the day I ever met you. To do this to not only those people, but to Big Pearl?" She pointed to Big Pearl. "One of the kindest people in this town? Someone who would've built your darn shed for free if only you'd asked. I don't know what else to say. I can't stay here." Fiona stomped out the room. "I can't stay here!"

"Fiona!"

Fiona did her best to block out Charlie's screams as she ran upstairs.

CHAPTER TWELVE

"Fiona!" Charlie tried to run after her, but Big Pearl blocked him. "Peter, Peter, I'm sorry. I was going to take care of you! I was gonna give your family good money. I swear I was!"

"Keep your money, Mr. Charlie." Big Pearl shrugged. "I don't want nothing from you, not even to share the air you breathe. I'm quittin' so you can get somebody else to do your shed."

Charlie dropped his head, whimpering.

"Miss Katherine, Miss Jane," Big Pearl said. "I apologize for wrecking yo' evening. Good night."

Charlie muttered, "Big Pearl."

He left.

"Damn it." Charlie turned away from everyone's gazes. "I'm sorry."

"Sorry don't keep those people in their homes, Charlie." Katherine raised her head. "I can honestly say I've never been more disappointed with you than I am now. Your father was ruthless, but Leonard had compassion. He wouldn't have ever done anything like this."

"Yeah, he had compassion all right." Charlie scoffed. "For everyone but *me*. My Fiona." He sucked back tears. "I've lost my Fiona forever."

"*Your* Fiona?" Jane pushed him. "What about me? The embarrassment you've caused! No way I'll marry you now. Laying down with that Negro woman? How dare you?" She slapped him. "You made a fool out of me! You can keep your wedding proposal and whatever else you had planned for us and stick it where the sun don't shine. I never wanna see you again, Charlie Bernstein. Never!" Jane marched out of the kitchen.

Sue Ann walked in wearing her gown and robe. "Squeaky-voice is leaving? She almost knocked me down in the hallway."

"Not now, Sue Ann." Charlie leaned over a chair, reflecting on the mess he made. "Go on back to your room if you got something smart to say."

"Hey, I'm thankful for whatever happened down here." She grabbed Jane's glass of champagne and drank. "Anything that gets Jane out of here is all right by me."

Jane stomped back inside. "I need a coachman to take me home!"

"Of course," Katherine said. "I apologize. We'll get you someone right now."

Katherine left, with Jane muttering in behind her.

"Is the engagement over?" Sue Ann laughed. "Another reason to drink up."

"There was no engagement and never will be one," Charlie said. "I gotta talk to Fiona and make this right—"

"She's not here." Sue Ann sat at the table, grabbing Jane's half-eaten queen cake. "She left."

Mildred batted her eyes. "What do you mean, she left?"

"She was in her room babbling about how she couldn't stay here in good conscience." She licked frosting from her thumb. "Oh, and how she'd rather eat out of a trash heap than to stay here with Charlie."

"Where'd she go?" Charlie hit the table. "Damn you, Sue Ann. Tell me where she went!"

"I don't know. But if she's gone, it's your own fault and you deserve it. Fiona's too good for you." She slurped more wine. "She took one of the horses. Didn't even pack up anything. Boy, Big Brother, you really have done it this time."

"Shut up, you ingrate!" He pushed her chair as he ran out of the dining room.

Katherine came down the hall.

"Momma, she's gone." Charlie stopped Katherine. "Fiona's left the house."

"Oh, dear God. In the middle of the night? She doesn't know her way around well enough."

"I gotta go." He raced past his mother. "Call the sheriff!"

"Where are you *going*?"

"To find the woman I love!" He ran. "I just hope it's not too late."

****

Nearly three hours later, Charlie rode his horse back through the woods near his estate. He'd seen more of Clear Creek County today than he had his entire life. He spoke to everyone he could find and visited every place, including boarding houses, churches, the jailhouse, the saloon and even the brothels. No one had even seen Fiona, let alone could tell him where she went.

As his horse trotted through the woods, Charlie didn't know how he'd go on if he never saw

Fiona again. If he had the chance, he'd change everything up to that point. He'd have never gotten

involved with that business deal and he'd have shouted from the rooftops how much he loved Fiona.

He would do anything to see her again: crawl over cracked glass, eat dirt, and even mutilate himself if need be.

He looked up at the glowing moon peeking through the trees. "God, please. Please, just let

me see her one more time. Give me a chance to make it right."

He heard a horse in the distance.

"Fiona?" Charlie urged his horse to pick up his speed. "Fiona?" He looked all around, waving the lantern. "Fiona, is that you?"

"Mr. Charlie?" A light appeared as Jake Duke and his brother Roy emerged from the woods on horseback.

"Shit." Charlie lowered his lantern. "Jake, Roy, what are you doing here?"

"We heard you was looking for Miss Fiona," Roy said. "Thought we'd help you out, so we came out here."

"Thank you." Charlie swallowed. "How could she not be anywhere? Something is definitely wrong. Someone would've seen her."

Jake steadied his fidgety horse. "Have you looked around here good?"

"Nah, it's so dark, even with the lantern."

"Well, three is better than one, so won't hurt if we split up," Roy said. "We'll cover more ground."

"Yeah." Charlie spit. "You seen Sheriff Snow today?"

"I think he went to Braesville," Jake said. "Don't worry. If Miss Fiona is still in Clear Creek County, me and Roy will find her."

The men split up.

Charlie looked around for any sign that Fiona had been out there: footprints, an article of clothing and, unfortunately, even blood. Maybe she'd hurt herself, which explained why she disappeared.

"Y'all see anything?" Jake's voice rattled through the darkness.

"No!" Charlie and Roy yelled back in unison.

"Please keep looking, guys!" Charlie shouted. "I ain't leaving until I find her!" He rode on, waving his lantern to see as much of the woods as he could. "Fiona?"

He heard footsteps, but the rhythm of the gait didn't sound human.

Charlie's horse trotted toward the sound and suddenly a brown horse broke off toward him. And it wasn't just any horse. It was Jeremiah, one of Charlie's horses.

"Jeremiah!" Charlie jumped off his horse and ran to the anxious animal, grabbing the reins.

"Sh. It's okay, boy. I got'cha." Charlie pet Jeremiah's head and he calmed down. "Fiona must be over here. Fiona?" Charlie ran to where Jeremiah came from and found Fiona laying back on a tree, unconscious with a line of blood running from her head. "No!" Charlie dropped beside her and took her into his arms. "Fiona? Fiona, wake up, please!" He tapped her cheek. "Oh my God." He listened to her chest and thank God he heard a heartbeat. "Oh, honey, what happened? Fiona, wake up. Please. Jake! Roy, over here! Guys, help me, please!"

The brothers galloped to where Charlie was and leapt off their horses.

"Is she okay?" Jake asked.

"No, does she look okay?" Charlie snapped. "She hit her head. She's bleeding!"

Roy touched the back of Fiona's head. "She hit it good, too."

"I think she was flung off Jeremiah." Charlie shook sweat from his face. "He probably got spooked by something and threw her off. I gotta get her back to the house."

"I don't think you should move her," Roy said. "Not supposed to move somebody with a head injury."

"I'm not gonna leave her out here." Grunting, Charlie scooped Fiona into his arms. "You guys go get Dr. Cassidy for me."

Jake and Roy nodded and ran back to their horses.

Holding Fiona, Charlie walked briskly with the horses trotting obediently beside him. "Get the doctor, boys. Hurry!"

CHAPTER THIRTEEN

Charlie put Fiona in his bedroom. He refused to lay her anywhere else. Then, he just sat there for moments, hours. He couldn't say. Time passed for everyone else, but not him. He just sat beside that bed, holding Fiona's limp hand and praying that his lie hadn't cost the woman he loved her life.

The door creaked open and Katherine walked in with another cup of tea, despite him telling her several times he didn't want any.

"Charlie, honey, you need to at least drink something."

"I want nothing." He stroked Fiona's hand. "She isn't waking up, Ma. Why isn't she waking up?"

"She's gonna be okay."

"Where's the damn doctor? He should've been here ages ago."

"He's the only one in the county, so he's probably busy. I'm sure he'll be here as soon as he can be."

"Probably not coming on purpose." He rocked. "He doesn't care about a Negro maid. Fiona's right. That's all people see her as, and I was as bad as them because I didn't stick up for her." He looked at Katherine with tears in his eyes. "I love Fiona, Momma. I love her with all my heart. I don't care she's colored or a maid and if I could marry her, I would."

"I know." Katherine's eyebrows drew together in the center. "You can't blame yourself—"

"The hell I can't! She's laying here because of my lies. Damn it!" He sniffed. "Why do I keep messing stuff up? No wonder I can't find genuine happiness and love, because I don't deserve it. I'm an awful person."

"Stop it, Charlie. I won't let you beat yourself up like this."

"What kind of man tries to kick people out of their homes? And then lies to the woman he loves and strings along another one?"

83

"You're a good person, Charlie. You'd never have been able to go through with that business deal. It would've eaten you alive."

"What's so bad is it disgusted me to do it, but I ignored my morals and did it, anyway."

"The deal hasn't happened yet. You can stop it."

"And I will." He kissed Fiona's hand. "I swear on Fiona's name that I'm gonna put all my time

and effort into building things people need, not a hotel, to line my pockets. And I'm gonna start with the Negros. I'm gonna build a brand new school for the colored children and a Negro clinic, too."

Katherine gaped.

"I'm gonna donate to stuff they need. It's the only way I can make up for what I almost did. Fiona was right. A house is more than just a place to live, and I'll never forgive myself for ignoring that."

Sue Ann waltzed in. "How is she doing?"

"We don't know," Katherine said. "I hope Dr. Cassidy gets here soon. I'll go keep watch for him." She hurried from the room.

Charlie squeezed Fiona's hand. "Please wake up, sweetheart. I promise I'll give you anything you want and I'll be a better man. Just don't leave me, Fiona." Charlie lifted his head, cursing himself. "Boy, did I drop the ball this time, huh? Be happy, Sue Ann. I'm the biggest loser in the family and not you. I always have been."

"Stop it."

"It's true." He sat back. "Other than making money, I can't do nothing right. I've been walking around saying I wish I could find true love and what do I do when I get it? I lie, scheme and try to kick people out of their homes. You need to get away from me, Sue Ann. Before I ruin your life, too."

"It might sound strange, but I believe in family sticking together and we're family." She smiled. "We might not get along all the time, but we're family and we always will be."

"You know what I like about you?"

She batted her eyelashes. "Is there anything?"

He chuckled. "You're genuine. I love how you don't care what anyone thinks about you. I wish I could be that courageous, but I'm not."

"Don't beat yourself up, Big Brother." She touched Fiona's head bandage. "We come from different worlds. You were born to privilege, and people expect different things from you. I'm sorry, Charlie."

"For what?"

"For being such a bitch." She pushed her hair off her shoulders. "Seeing Fiona like this

reminds me how important family is. I'm sick of fighting and always being upset."

"And drinking? Drinking only makes things worse."

"I know. But what do you do when liquor becomes your best friend?" She shrugged. "Pathetic, but it's true."

"I'm sorry, Little Sister. For all the pain my father ever caused you. And any time I made you feel unwanted in this house. You are a Bernstein in every sense of the word."

She exhaled.

"From now on, I'm gonna be the best big brother you could ever ask for." Charlie reached over Fiona and took Sue Ann's hand. "I love you, Sue Ann."

She gaped as if someone had pulled a gun on her.

"I never said it before." He nodded. "But I do."

Her eyes filled with tears. "I think that's the first time anyone's ever said they loved me."

Charlie smiled. "It won't be the last."

****

Thank goodness Dr. Cassidy came when he did, because Charlie had done nothing right. He figured he probably shouldn't have moved Fiona so quickly, but how could he leave her laying there in the woods like that? Turns out Fiona had a concussion, so moving her had been his first mistake.

Second, Charlie and Katherine had put the bandage on too tight, and hadn't known to keep Fiona's extremities warm.

Cassidy set a bed warmer and hot water bottles under the sheet to provide adequate warmth

at least until morning. "Okay, that should keep her warm enough. You have to check this and make sure her bed is warm, okay, Charlie? It's very important she stays warm through this."

Charlie nodded, sitting beside the bed. "So no more hand holding?"

"Not unless your hand is as warm as those water bottles, no." Cassidy zipped up his bulky leather bag and took off his glasses.

Shoot, Charlie couldn't guess how old Dr. Jack Cassidy was. It was like a running joke in the town, no one really knew. He'd been the doctor of Clear Creek County since before Charlie was born. And he assumed the decrepit, moving-slower-than-a-snail physician might've been practicing when Leonard and Katherine were children as well.

But again, no one cared how old Cassidy was. The town praised him because despite his

faults, he was the only doctor in town, which in their eyes made him close to God.

"She needs to stay in bed for at least a week." Cassidy sat up straight, barely taller than the little saplings in Charlie's yard. He seemed to shrink a foot each year. "I will come back then and check on her. If you have any problems before then, call me."

"Thank you so much, Doctor." Charlie stood and took Cassidy's wrinkled old hand. "I'm just happy she's gonna be okay."

"Head injuries are tricky." Cassidy looked at Fiona. "But the rest of her is fine. You just gotta keep watch over her."

"Oh, I will." Charlie flattened his hand to his chest, making a vow. "I won't even leave this room until she wakes up. Do you know how long that will be?"

Cassidy shook his head. "These things are impossible to pinpoint. Could be tonight and could be next week. We can't rush healing. She'll awaken when it's time."

"Yeah." Charlie held in tears of guilt and fear. "Thanks again, Dr. Cassidy. Miss Mildred?"

She rushed into the room.

"Please show Dr. Cassidy to his carriage."

"Yes, sir." Mildred smiled. "Follow me, Doctor Cassidy."

Cassidy nodded at Charlie one last time before he left.

"My sweet Fiona." Charlie sat back by the bed, dying to hold her hand but couldn't. "Please, wake up. Just not seeing your eyes and hearing your voice is killing me. I'm sorry for everything I did." He touched her warm cheek. "When you wake up, I'll make this all up to you, Fiona. I promise."

He laid his head on the edge of the bed and fell asleep.

CHAPTER FOURTEEN

After an entire night of alternate sleeping and praying and Charlie watching over Fiona like the angel she was, the sweetest sound greeted him as he awoke the next morning: Fiona moaning.

Charlie jerked forward in the chair, his blanket slipping onto the floor. He'd slept in his shirt and trousers and even his shoes. "Fiona?"

"Huh?" She licked her lips, prying her eyes open. "Ah."

"Too much light?" Charlie ran to the window and closed the curtain. "How's that?"

She groaned, moving her head against the pillow. "Ow."

"Easy." He ran to her. "Don't move too much, okay? You have a concussion."

"What's that?"

"A head injury. Dr. Cassidy says you'll be okay, but you need rest."

"I'm so hot." She wiggled her arms and legs under the sheet. "Is it a bed warmer under here?"

"Yep, and leave it alone. You gotta stay warm for your head to heal."

"God." She swallowed. "My throat is so dry."

Charlie grabbed the jug of water and poured some into the cup he'd been drinking out of all night. "Here. You need help?"

She nodded.

Slowly, Charlie eased her head up enough for her to drink.

Fiona took long, sloppy sips as if she hadn't had water in a hundred years. "Oh, my head." She lay back down. "I feel awful. So exhausted. My head's pounding and my jaw is sore."

"I found you laying in the woods with Jeremiah. Do you know what happened?"

"He got spooked." She struggled to swallow. "A deer ran in front of him. He bucked and threw me off. I don't know what happened after that."

"You hit your head on a tree. Fiona, you're lucky to be alive."

"You... you found me?" Her face lit up despite the pain she was obviously in. "You went after me when I left?"

"Course I did. After all, it was my fault you left."

She blinked, slowly.

"I've said I love you many times already. Now I'm gonna show you. I'm gonna do right by

you, Fiona. I'm gonna do right by Big Pearl and everyone else in West Pine, too."

She flinched. "How?"

"The deal is off. Instead of tearing down West Pine, I'm gonna make it better. I wanna build a colored school and a clinic. Both will be the best they can be."

"Charlie." She flinched from moving too quickly. "That's so touching."

"I feel awful, Fiona." He looked at the floor. "Ma was right. I couldn't have gone through with that deal in the end. It's not me."

"It isn't." She grabbed his hand.

"No, you gotta keep your hands warm."

"If I can't touch *you*, then what's the point of even waking up?"

He smiled, relief flooding his body.

"I'm sorry too," she said.

"What for? You did nothing."

"Maybe it's the concussion, but it's got me thinking about when we were in the garden after I first saw you with Jane, and you told me about how Leonard treated you. I didn't show you an inch of compassion, Charlie."

"I didn't deserve any after I hurt you like that."

"No, I was wrong. I love you and I should've listened. Now I understand you. You've never known real love, have you, Charlie?"

He shifted his gaze away from her.

"Out of all your money and sophistication, actual love is the one thing you've never had. I'm sorry your father made you feel like property instead of his son. Something to groom and build instead of someone to nurture and love. Well, look at me, Charlie." She squeezed his hand as he looked into her eyes. "I love you, Charlie. *I* love you and I always will."

"Oh, Fiona." Charlie leaned over and gave her a timid kiss to not cause her any pain.

Fiona rejected the tenderness, threw her arm around his shoulders, and kissed him with such vigor it felt even better than making love to her. Like that first hit from a pipe stuffed with the freshest tobacco.

"Mm." Charlie kept his eyes closed afterwards and didn't dare lick his lips, for he wanted her taste to linger. "That was the best kiss I've ever had."

She chuckled. "There's more where that came from. If you want it."

"Oh I want it, Fiona." He hugged her. "That and *more*."

THE END

To receive book announcements subscribe to Stacy's mailing list:

Mailing List[1]

---

1. https://stacybooks.eo.page/cjjy6

Don't miss out!

Visit the website below and you can sign up to receive emails whenever Stacy-Deanne publishes a new book. There's no charge and no obligation.

https://books2read.com/r/B-A-RTFC-DOXAC

BOOKS 2 READ

Connecting independent readers to independent writers.

Also by Stacy-Deanne

Billionaires For Black Girls
Billionaire for the Night
Billionaire Takes the Bride
Billionaire At 36k Feet
Billionaire's Love Trap
Billionaire in the Caribbean
Billionaire Broken
Billionaire Times Two

Sex in the Wild West Series
Maid for Two
Fling on the Frontier
Favor for His Wife
The Carriage Ride

Stripped Romantic Suspense Series
Stripped
Captured
Damaged
Haunted

Possessed
Destined
Stripped Series (Books 1-5)
Stripped Series Books 1-3
Stripped Series (Books 4-6)

Tate Valley Romantic Suspense Series
Now or Never
Now or Never
Chasing Forever
Chasing Forever
Sinner's Paradise
Sinner's Paradise
Last Dance
Last Dance
Tate Valley The Complete Series

The Bruised Series
Bruised
Captivated
Disturbed
Entangled
Twisted

The Good Girls and Bad Boys Series
Who's That Girl?
You Know My Name
Hate the Game

Bruised Complete Series

Tate Valley Complete Series

The Princess and the Thief

The Little Girl

The Stranger

Oleander

Seducing Her Father's Enemy

Love & Murder: 3-Book Romantic Suspense Starter Set

Paradise

Stalked by the Quarterback

Stripped Complete Series

Tell Me You Love Me

Secrets of the Heart

Five Days

Off the Grid

Sex in Kenya

Fatal Deception

A Cowboy's Debt

Billionaires for Black Girls Set (1-4)

A Savior for Christmas

The Samsville Setup

Trick The Treat

The Cowboy She Left in Wyoming

Theodore's Ring

Wrangle Me, Cowboy

The Billionaire's Slave

The Cowboy's Twin

Everwood County Plantation

Billionaires for Black Girls Set 5-7

The Lonely Hearts of San Sity

Stranded with Billionaire Grumpy Pants